Echoland

ALSO BY PER PETTERSON

To Siberia
In the Wake
Out Stealing Horses
I Curse the River of Time
It's Fine By Me
Ashes in My Mouth, Sand in My Shoes
I Refuse

Per Petterson

Echoland

TRANSLATED
FROM THE NORWEGIAN
BY

Don Bartlett

Harvill *Secker*
LONDON

1 3 5 7 9 10 8 6 4 2

Harvill Secker, an imprint of Vintage,
20 Vauxhall Bridge Road,
London SW1V 2SA

Harvill Secker is part of the Penguin Random House group of companies whose
addresses can be found at global.penguinrandomhouse.com.

This book was published with the financial assistance of NORLA

Published with the support of the Creative Europe Programme of the European Union

The European Commission support for the production of this publication
does not constitute an endorsement of the contents which reflects
the views only of the author, and the Commission cannot be held
responsible for any use which may be made of the information
contained therein

First published with the title *Ekkoland* in Norway by Forlaget Oktober in 1989

www.vintage-books.co.uk

A CIP catalogue record for this book is available from the British Library

ISBN 9781846554490

Typeset by Palimpsest Book Production Ltd, Falkirk, Stirlingshire
Printed and bound by Clays Ltd, St Ives plc

Penguin Random House is committed to a sustainable
future for our business, our readers and our planet.
This book is made from Forest Stewardship
Council® certified paper.

CONTENTS

Jutland, Jutland
oh, land of earth and air, of boundless space
with splendour in your light,
age imprinted on your lips,
the sea's broad panoply
above your beaches
at a distance, solitude.
Oh, Echoland, where the air
has hidden traces, has answers,
rye-white land, my childhood's hapless abode
giddy with air and earth.

Paul la Cour

THE COAST ROSE, BUT NOT BY MUCH

They sailed across the sea to Denmark. Along the fjord the bonfires lit up the summer evening and Arvid stood by the railing gazing towards land, pretending they were stars. The lights rose and fell and they shone on the water and he heard laughter and singing from the shore, but the ship was quiet.

The ship was called the *Vistula* and had been named after a river in Poland. Arvid had never been to Poland, but before they were past Nesodden his father had told the story about the man who was going to America on board the *Stavanger Fjord*. The engine packed up almost at once and they had to sail round Hovedøya island back to the harbour and then the man was standing on deck shouting in an American accent to those who hadn't yet left the quay: 'Is my old mother still alive?' But Arvid had heard the story so many times before and only his father laughed.

The white houses sank and withdrew into the country-side and slowly the fjord grew wider. The *Vistula* passed Drøbak and sailed on through the sound where the wreck of the battleship *Blücher* lay on the seabed by Oscarsborg fortress. They had sailed over it and perhaps the dead bodies were still there. The skies turned dark, but not by much, for it was Midsummer Night, and then it happened, what he was waiting for. The little boat from the town of Horten appeared from behind an island and chugged across the fjord in a wide arc. The noise from the *Vistula*'s engine went quiet until he could barely hear its thrumming, and the spray from the bows ceased. The *Vistula* glided through the water, waiting, and Arvid waited too. The little boat approached and turned until it was in line with the ship. Arvid could see the skipper at the helm and his white cap, and a couple were standing on the deck with a suitcase between them. The man was holding his hat and the woman was looking straight down.

There was a clang from the side of the ship and a gangway was extended from the hull. Arvid leaned further over and saw a hand stretched out below, and suddenly he felt a grip around his thigh. His whole body went cold and he turned quickly. He saw a man smiling.

'Fancy a late evening swim, do you? Be careful,' he said, with an even bigger smile. He had a hat on, and a coat, and he looked ordinary. 'You just watch, I will hold you.'

Arvid stared at him. In the end he said: 'You will *not*,' and turned away again. Now the little boat was up close, and they rocked towards each other and away again with the waves they themselves had made, and the man with the suitcase said, 'Now,' and stepped across. The outstretched hand helped him in and then it waved to the woman. She stared at the open water between the boats, which was no more than a thin strip, where the tyres the length of the Horten boat kept them apart.

'No,' she said in a loud voice, but the hand only waved more eagerly.

'No, you idiot!' she shouted. 'I don't want to!' And then Arvid could see who owned the hand for he leaned right over and grabbed the woman's shoulder and pulled her across.

'Idiot!' she screamed.

The man behind Arvid laughed and said: 'That was a bad start to the holiday. There must be easier ways of getting to Denmark.' He stood right by Arvid, and Arvid straightened up and moved away from the railing.

'What's your name?'

'Arvid Jansen.'

'How old are you?'

'Twelve. Almost.'

'You're a fine figure of a lad,' the man said, stroking Arvid's hair, and Arvid took a step back.

'No I am not. I'm Italian.'

'Is that right?' said the man, raising an eyebrow, for he knew nothing at all about Bruno Angelini, the baker's son from Naples who thought the city's streets were hot enough without having to stand in his father's bakery as well. It was as hot as hell there and Bruno longed to get

3

out to where the air didn't stand still and the eye could see further than the nearest stack of loaves. He could have become a fisherman or a labourer and chose the latter, at seventeen. He worked on roads for several years and then he worked on railways, when railways were stretching across Italy to hold the new state together. For this job strong men were required who would graft. Bruno was small, but he was strong and he could graft. He was going further and further away from Naples, and sometimes all he longed for was the glittering bay with Capri in the distance.

To the north there were more rivers and valleys and ravines, and bridges had to be built. Bruno built bridges. Soon there was no type of bridge he hadn't worked on, and when a call went out for experienced labourers to build a railway bridge across the Limfjord in Denmark, in the far north, Bruno was among those who signed up. Arvid's history book told of a Europe emerging from several wars, and travelling north was not without dangers. But Bruno set off, and in the spring of 1874 he found accommodation in Ålborg on the Limfjord.

It took almost five years. When the bridge was finished four Italians had died, five Frenchmen and many others had life-changing injuries. Bruno was the foreman of a five-man team and most of the time they worked under-water, in pressure chambers where three of them dug the mud and two sent it up a shaft. Above them the huge

4

pillars were built with hard-baked bricks and they felt heavy on Bruno's shoulders and neck.

In 1879 all the guest workers went back home, except Bruno. He wanted to see the Danish king open the bridge, and he had grown fond of the country with the low coastline, although his respect for Danish engineers had diminished.

King Christian took the train from Ålborg to Nørresundby on the northern side of the Limfjord. He was supposed to walk back and open the bridge, but the rain came down and the wind picked up, so he took the train back again, and from Ålborg station he crossed in a coach which brought him dry-shod to the opening ceremony.

'Useless monarch!' Bruno said, standing among the Danish workers.

Now he was finished with bridges. But he didn't return home, he went even further north. In the fishing village of Bangsbostrand he met a girl who was blonde and her name was Lotte, and so he became a fisherman after all. But that was all fine for it wasn't so hot here and even a short man could see a long distance in Northern Jutland and the air was never still. In each generation after him there was one Italian, and when Arvid thought about him he saw an open, tanned face with dark curls above it, and that's how Arvid himself looked, and what he didn't know about Bruno, he made up. And he thought, you don't *have* to be Norwegian, you can be something else, somewhere else other than Oslo.

You can be an Italian in Denmark. You can leave your own skin and be whoever you like and no one can get near you. Not everyone was brave enough to do this, but Arvid was, and the man in the hat and coat could understand nothing of this. Arvid took another step back and then Gry called to him from the deck above, where she was standing with his mother. The man looked up at them and back down at Arvid and touched his hat as if to another adult and went into the cafeteria.

'Who was that?' Gry said afterwards.

'It was just a man.'

He was allowed to stay up until they passed Færder lighthouse at the mouth of the fjord, which was creepy and lonesome and seductive as it swung its arms round in the night, and then he had to go down to bed. But it was warm inside and the stairs were steep and had banisters of mahogany and brass, there was the smell of engine room and beef in the corridors and inside the cabin there were china pots in the cupboard under the sink. They were for pissing in at night, but after Færder they mostly came out when someone had to throw up.

When his father turned off the light it was pitch black and Arvid didn't know whether he was asleep or awake for when he opened his eyes he saw as little as he did when he had them closed. He lay there in the night that wrapped itself around him and became a world of its own and felt the boat lift him up, press against his stomach and let him fall, and he smiled in the darkness and heard his father groan on the lower bunk. There was a creak every time he turned to stop himself throwing up.

'I know you're grinning, Arvid! Pack it in!' his father's voice said, and Arvid couldn't hold it back any longer and laughed out loud.

In the morning he awoke and went up on deck with Gry. They leaned over the railing and let the wind tousle their hair until it felt soaked in Vaseline and thick to the touch, and they threw Marie biscuits to the gulls sailing like white crosses above the boat, and they dived to catch them, and only one biscuit fell into the sea.

Then Arvid and Gry went in and had breakfast in the cafeteria and sat talking and thinking until they could see the island with the lighthouse through the windows. They went back out and watched the wake as the ship turned in towards land. The coast rose, but not by much, for it was Denmark and the ship glided quietly through the opening in the mole, past the fishing cutters with their masts stripped of their sails like a winter forest, and Grandfather stood on the quay in his brown beret and equally brown moustache. His blue moped was parked by the harbour shed, and when Grandfather spotted them he raised his arm very slowly and waved his hand. Arvid had never seen him make a sudden movement.

They waved back and his father saw the moped and

had *that* expression round his mouth and everyone knew what he was going to say.

'Dad, you haven't even got a moped,' Gry said and so his father said nothing and Arvid thought the moped was great and the town was small, so what use was a car to Grandfather?

They took their bikes and suitcases from the *Vistula* and Grandfather tied the biggest case to the luggage rack on his moped. Then they set off across the harbour square, past the Ferry Inn, which was a low dive, up Lodsgade a few blocks to the house where LODSGADE DAIRY was written above the shop windows on the ground floor. It was Grandmother's shop, and there were white tiles on the walls and on the counter and in the window there were cheeses on display that Arvid would never have dreamed of eating, just the thought of it made him feel sick. But along one wall there was a line of jars with crystallised fruits in them and sweets called rusty frogs and it felt good to stand behind the counter when the Danish kids came in the door with their five-øre coins because he knew they thought he could help himself whenever he liked.

When they arrived, Grandmother was standing in the arch leading to the courtyard with her eyes so blue they could see right through you and out to the mission fields in Africa, and she gave a limp smile when she hugged Arvid. That was because they had come so early she hadn't put her false teeth in yet. Arvid could see that and he thought it was disgusting. He walked past her and up the steep spiral staircase to the first floor where the little kitchen was to the left, the living room straight ahead and the bedroom behind it, and that was all there was.

'Welcome to Denmark, welcome my dears,' Grandmother said.

'Sure,' said Mum, and her voice was as shiny and taut as a wire and Arvid stopped to listen, but she didn't say anything more that he could hear.

Every time they came here with the ship, Grandfather moved to the divan in the living room and Grandmother to the little room behind the dairy shop which was so small they called it the Aquarium. It was almost entirely white, there were white lace curtains and white roller blinds in the window, there was a white crocheted frilly cover on the divan and a frame on the wall proclaiming JESUS LIVES in white embroidered Gothic letters.

Everyone was glad Arvid had stopped wetting the bed. More so as the whole family used to sleep in the double bed with the carved headboard, for Grandfather was a cabinetmaker, and it wasn't funny to wake up in the morning and pretend you were still asleep and hear his father hiss in a low voice: 'Goddamn it, will this never end!' and then to feel his mother stroking his hair, because she always knew when he wasn't sleeping, and hear her say: 'Come on, Frank, you know he can't help it. He'll soon grow out of it. Besides, he has troubles of his own. You should think about that!'

Arvid wondered about him having troubles of his own, but he didn't know what she meant, and in the end he forgot to think about it.

DON'T YOU TOUCH ME

He woke up next morning and crawled down to the foot of the bed. From there he had to jump over Gry, who was sleeping on a mattress on the floor. This year she was too big to lie in the middle with Arvid, she said, and she was right, she would soon be fourteen, would be starting *realskole* in the autumn, and she had very long legs.

He braced himself, jumped and flew into the living room, tripped over the high threshold and landed spreadeagled on one of Grandmother's home-made rugs.

'Hell!' he shouted as his elbow hit the floor and he looked up and there was Grandfather with a smirk under his moustache.

'Are you coming?' he said, and Arvid nodded, because that was exactly what he wanted.

They walked quietly down the stairs and into the shop. The sun angled through the windows and made everything in the room shockingly white. Arvid blinked and leaned over the edge of the cooler chest and began to take out bottles. They were in water up to their necks. His stomach contracted and froze, he shivered, and then he heard Grandmother crying behind the closed Aquarium door.

He glanced at Grandfather, but Grandfather just shrugged in irritation and went out through the door carrying a box of shiny milk bottles.

It was Arvid who delivered milk to the customers who lived higher than the ground floor. He ran up the stairs with a bottle under each arm, they were cold in his armpits, but it was fine because almost no houses in this town had more than four storeys, and the people who lived in them had names like Straarup and Olesen and Kærstrand and Maltesen, but never Pettersen.

The round took him just half an hour. There weren't that many customers now as the new supermarket was finished down at the harbour, and the round ended at Gammeltorv. Another shop's territory started there and you had to respect boundaries, Grandfather said, although he stared longingly up at the hospital, which stood opposite and got through an ocean of milk every day.

Grandfather took a small shiny box out of his pocket and removed something round and black, from which he cut a chunk with his penknife.

'Want to try, Arvid?' he said, holding out the black roll to Arvid after helping himself.

'I'm only twelve, just about,' Arvid said, 'I'm not allowed to.'

'But it's just like liquorice,' Grandfather said, and it did look like liquorice, so he said yes, and Grandfather cut him off a bit and put it in his mouth.

At first it tasted vile, like horse muck, he thought, although he didn't know what horse muck tasted like, and then it began to burn and sting his tongue, he could feel the heat rising in his face, he couldn't breathe and he spat the clump out, but it ran in a thick stream down his chest, over the Hawaiian shirt he had been given by Aunt Kari, who said he looked like Elvis when he combed his wet hair and put it on.

Grandfather stared at him and burst into laughter, he laughed so much he had to lean on the delivery bike, he stared at the sky, and then he closed his eyes, removed his glasses and wiped his face, he had laughed so much. Arvid had never heard laughter like it, it was funny and infectious, and he wished they could share what had made his grandfather laugh. That he too could lean against his bike and laugh and look up at the sky and wipe his face and tell his mother and father about it afterwards, so that they too could laugh, as they usually did when something was really funny. But this wasn't funny, he ran the back of his hand across his mouth and it went a brownish-black and sticky and he felt like crying. But he didn't want to cry in front of his grandfather, so he said: 'Damn, damn, damn,' as loud as he dared.

On their way home they stopped by the bus station, where there was an ice machine in the middle of the square, and his grandfather put two kroner in the slot and a big block of ice slid down, and it was so cold you would burn your hands if you touched it. Grandfather wrapped it in coarse sacking and put it in the front of the Long John delivery bike.

'If you lean against it you'll get a cold shoulder,' he said, and burst into laughter again, but Arvid kept his distance, for the ice was as hard as a diamond and cold as the North Pole, and with a shiver he felt the goose-pimples spreading, and his grandfather cycled as fast as he could to get home before the ice started melting in the sun. Back in the shop, he put it in the box on top of the ice chest. Then they went up to have breakfast with the others.

Grandmother came from the kitchen with the large coffee pot in one hand while the other tried to catch a loose lock of hair from the bun at the back of her head. Her mouth was fine now, but her eyes were red-rimmed as she poured the coffee and milk into Arvid's cup. Gry was squirming on her chair and his mother was staring stiffly out of the window. Finally she turned to Arvid and said: 'Look at you, boy! Go and change your shirt!'

Arvid rose from the table, went into the bedroom, tugged off the Hawaiian shirt and slung it into the corner with as much force as he could. He rummaged through the suitcase and found the Texas shirt, put it on and went back to the table.

After breakfast Grandfather went to his workshop to finish a dresser he had promised for the day before.

14

'No children allowed,' he said, and was gone down the stairs.

They cleared the table and Gry and his mother went to help Grandmother in the shop and his father and Arvid fetched their bikes. They cycled down Lodsgade, alongside the harbour and headed out of town. Frydenstrand Hotel towered up behind a scruffy willow hedge and was white and ghost-like, with boarded-up windows, and Arvid was glad to turn away from it and into Strandvejen. The tall poplar trees rose above them, sunlight filtered through the foliage forming yellow pools on the tarmac, and they cycled right through them, and the sea spread out vast and grey in the distance, and ahead of them stood the lighthouse on the low island and was a raised index finger on the horizon. The old kiosk wasn't open yet, so they cycled past it, and past the jetty and right out to where the tarmac ended and the gravel road began. There they dropped their bikes in the lyme grass and walked down to the beach. It was wide and a greyish-brown, stretching as far as he could see, and was lovelier than anywhere else he had been.

Arvid's father held his hand, and although it was embarrassing, Arvid didn't pull his hand away. Behind them they left two lines of footprints, one big and one small, Robinson Crusoe and Man Friday out scouting to see if a ship would come and take them off this godforsaken island. But it wasn't an island, it was Denmark and the lighthouse didn't quite fit the scene.

Along the beach a belt of rushes rippled in the wind, like a green river, like the Mississippi in *Huckleberry Finn*, if you thought about it and wanted it enough, and whenever you walked back from the beach, you could see the mouth of a creek dividing the rushes, and there were small boats lying there reflected in a zigzag pattern in the brackish water.

He tore himself from his father's hand and ran up the beach, turned so fast the sand flared out, and he ran back and said in a breathless voice: 'Dad?'

Yes?'

'I need a pee.'

'Just have a pee then. You can go to the edge of the rushes and pee. That's a good place.'

Arvid went to the edge of the rushes and peed. It was nice to pee outdoors. He only did it in the summer and only when he was here.

'Peeing outdoors is being on holiday,' Dad said, looking as if he had just proclaimed one of the Ten Commandments, from where he stood smoking a cigarette and gazing at the lighthouse. Then he threw the butt into a wave that lapped up against the shore, almost reaching their feet before retreating. The cigarette went out with a hiss and Arvid's father said: 'If you ever start smoking, Arvid, you must do what I do. Only smoke in the holidays because smoking damages your body and you shouldn't let that happen. Your body is a gift.'

16

'I know,' Arvid said, and then he said, 'Oh no!'

'What's up?'

'I peed a bit in my trousers when I was doing up my flies.'

'Never mind. You know what they say: no matter how hard you shake your peg, the last drop goes down your leg.'

His father laughed and Arvid laughed too, although he didn't think it was all that funny and when he saw from his father's face that he thought it was extremely funny, he could feel himself blushing.

It was out here he first realised he could swim. One day he just fell forward into the water and moved his arms and legs and he was off. So long as he kept his back arched and didn't lose his nerve he was fine, but his mother, who saw what he was doing, said: 'That's all very good, Arvid, but don't you ever swim beyond the third sandbank, there are dangerous riptides out there!' And she told him about the German tourist who had been showing off and hadn't listened to what people said. He had been caught by a riptide and pulled down to the bottom. They never found him, his mother said, and it happened just after the War, so God knows how hard they tried.

The following nights Arvid dreamed about the German who disappeared: a white arm sticking out of the sea in the distance and him standing on land shouting: '*Achtung,*

17

Schweinehund!' again and again, which were the only words in German he knew.

But that was several years ago, it was low tide now and the first two sandbanks rose from the sea. From afar they looked like the crests of waves, but up close the sea was still, and above what appeared to be the tips of the waves, there were long lines of gulls strutting along on dry land.

He got up from the rock they were sitting on and ran into the water, gym shoes and all. He waved his arms and shouted and the white birds took off and merged into flapping clouds making one hell of a racket. He screamed and the gulls screamed back and began to circle like a tornado, he leaned back and looked up and it was wonderful, but as he waded back across the shallows, his mouth felt dry, his trousers were soaking wet and inside his shoes wet sand chafed against the soles of his feet.

'Damn it, Arvid, couldn't you have taken your shoes off first?' his father said, but Arvid shrugged and answered: 'Why is Grandmother crying?'

'What do you mean?'

'Why is Grandmother crying and why does Mum get so angry every time we come here?'

'Do they? I haven't noticed,' his father said and blushed, and he looked very uncomfortable.

'Right, sure you haven't,' Arvid said, and walked towards his bike, picked it up, climbed on and cycled down the gravel road. It was difficult to stay upright because nothing had been done to this road for at least twenty years. There were rocks sticking up that caught the wheels, he almost came off, and he was barely round the first bend and there, straight ahead on a field, a hare was sitting with its ears sticking up like two antennae.

He stopped and left the bike in the ditch, lay down and began to crawl across the field. The hare watched him, but it didn't move, and very silently he drew closer and slowly stretched out his arm, and he said so softly in a tone of voice he had never heard himself use before: 'Hey, little hare, hey, come over here.' He reached out his arm and held it there for a long time, and it wasn't heavy because he put all his strength into the arm until it glowed and felt like a magnet, and the hare jumped twice and was suddenly very close, its nose touched his hand, he made a grab for it and the hare shot off towards the beach like a bullet. He let his arm fall, and his face sank into the sandy earth.

There was the clatter of a bike behind him.

'Hey, Arvid, what *are* you doing?'

'Nothing,' he murmured into the ground, and his lips were covered in sand, and he heard his father put down his bike and stride across the grass. A shadow fell over his body and he felt his father's hand on his head.

'Hey, come on, what's up?' his father said, and Arvid jumped up spitting sand, and he yelled:

'Don't you touch me!'

TORO! TORO!

Arvid and Mogens raced along the road by the beach. Arvid on his second-hand Svithun and Mogens on his standard black Danish boneshaker with the laughably small luggage rack. They stopped at the old kiosk and each bought a Giant Eskimo and pedalled on with one hand holding the ice cream and the other pointing to the sky, which was fine because the bikes themselves knew where they were going. The chocolate ice cream tasted cold and good and vaguely of seaweed, and they heard the wind in the poplars and the distant voices of shimmering shapes against the light walking in the shallows with forks and buckets digging for fat worms in the sand that had just been exposed.

The sea could be grey or green or close to brown, but today it was shiny and blue, and that meant it wasn't so warm. But the sun was boiling hot, and the sky and the ocean merged on the horizon, and you couldn't see where one finished and the other started, it was like a huge silk blanket, soft and cool, and if you were close to your body and you weren't fat or old, but were a boy and had your body wrapped tight around you, you could throw yourself into that blanket with all your strength and return just as whole.

And that's what they did. They jumped off their bikes as they were still moving and let them carry on until they toppled over and landed in the grass next to each other, and Arvid and Mogens changed into bathing trunks while eating what was left of the ice cream. They ran along the brown rotting timbers of the old jetty that they feared might collapse beneath them and as they dived from the edge they threw the lolly sticks which hung like butterflies in all the blue.

Mogens was thirteen and a half, and Arvid first met him in the toilet. He had taken the key from the bottom of the stairs and walked across the yard, but when he was about to turn the key he saw the door wasn't locked, so he opened it and there was Mogens sitting on the toilet with his trousers down below his knees, reading a magazine.

'Hi, my name's Mogens,' Mogens said. 'Have you read this? What rubbish!' He waved the newspaper and Arvid could see it was one of Grandmother's missionary magazines. He agreed; he had read papers that were more fun.

He went out to wait until Mogens was finished and when Mogens came out he said: 'Let's go for a swim.'

Then they went for a swim, and now they had done that so many times.

Mogens was taller than Arvid, his body was full of sinews and muscles, he was in a sports team at school and did loads of training, and when he wanted to point out something to Arvid, he placed the hand he wasn't pointing with on Arvid's shoulder and held it there until he had finished explaining. Arvid didn't know what to think about that, except that he could *feel* the hand, even after Mogens had removed it.

Mogens' father was a welder down at the shipyard, where they drank beer and aquavit in the lunch break, and Arvid liked Mogens so much because he came out with so many unexpected things and had such a tongue on him and could be so foul-mouthed with Arvid, without him taking offence. Mogens could cycle faster than Arvid, but Arvid was a better swimmer, and that was fine by Mogens.

'You idiot. I can see your bollocks!' Mogens was the first in the sea, he was treading water and stared right up into Arvid's crotch as Arvid came after him with a monster jump. Arvid didn't blush, because Mogens was the only person who could say 'bollocks' out loud without making him embarrassed, and Mogens was right of course, he had put on his trunks so quickly they weren't on straight, and he hit the sea with a happy snigger. He adjusted his trunks before he came up again to the surface.

'Hey, watch out for the jellyfish!' Mogens shouted, and Arvid rolled over like a seal, narrowly avoiding an orange creature the size of a serving platter. Fortunately the current was moving in the opposite direction and the stinging tentacles billowed past Arvid, and he thought, how strange that such a thing is alive.

They raced each other back to the beach under the jetty and Arvid counted the posts the whole way in, seeing nothing else, and he gave it all he had and when his belly scraped the sandy bottom he had swum past more than twenty and was several metres ahead.

They were sitting in the sun drying off, but the sun was cold and his body was slowly going stiff.

'Your back looks like a plucked chicken,' Mogens said. 'Let's run, come on!'

The beach was several kilometres long and they could run as far as they wanted, slowly at first for a good while, then a spurt, the heat pounding through their legs and up their backs to their shoulders, it was like oiling all the joints and their legs were going like pistons. There's nothing like being almost twelve years old, he thought, nothing! And he threw his arms into the air and shouted: '*Viva Garibaldi!*' to the sea and the island. Mogens came to a sudden halt in front of him and hurled him to the ground, they rolled around in the sand, which stuck to their sweaty stomachs, to their backs and legs, there was sand everywhere, it crunched between their teeth, and he tried to get a grip around Mogens' neck, but every time he got an arm round him, Mogens slipped away.

'Ha!' Mogens shouted, made a feint and wrestled Arvid to the ground. 'Do you surrender?'

'Never,' Arvid said, and started to laugh because he was quite stuck. 'You look like an old man,' he laughed. Mogens' hair was white and his eyebrows were bushy with sand. He brushed his hair and face and the sand drizzled down on to Arvid, who had to close his eyes and spit it out.

'Let's wash the sand off in the sea,' Mogens said. 'Last one in's a sissy.'

'OK,' Arvid said, but Mogens didn't move, just sat on top of him smiling, and then he laughed.

'OK!' He jumped up and raced to the sea without seeming tired at all. They swam underwater to get completely clean, jellyfish glided past like crystal balls and the sun shone back from the ridged sandy bottom. When they re-emerged their hair was slicked back and Mogens said: 'You look like a mafioso. Do you want to do some rowing?'

'Sure.'

'My father's got a boat nearby. We can row up the creek. You haven't been there before, have you?'

'No.'

'Great, wait here and I'll go and get it.' Mogens waded out of the water and jogged towards the rushes where the creek met the sea, and the boats were there. Arvid lay back and floated, the salty water lifted him up and down with the waves, he bobbed like a cork and then he stood up and walked back through the shallows.

He wasn't alone. Some distance away a man was jumping up and down in the water. The man was laughing out loud, and then Arvid saw the man wasn't on his own either. A knee stuck up on either side of his chest above the water and when the man turned Arvid saw her face against his neck. Her long dark hair hung straight down, heavy and wet. She was quite still, clinging to the man, and Arvid walked off through the water in the opposite direction, back to the rushes.

He knew he would turn round and look at them again, but he tried not to and pushed his hands down into the sand, dug as deep as he could and took them out again and all they brought up was sticky sand and small white shells that cut his palms. He was grey and sticky up to his elbows, so he went back to the water's edge to rinse his arms and then he turned and saw them running out of the sea. Water was dripping from their bodies, glinting in the sun and the blue, and then they sort of sank slowly to the beach and kissed each other, their legs intertwined, she was tanned while he was paler, it looked odd. He bit her ear and she stuck her tongue out and he took it in his mouth. Arvid held his breath. Then they sensed he was there and she lifted herself up on her elbows, dry white sand along the length of her brown arm and she called out teasingly: 'Hey, come here, boy!'

'Don't you touch me!' he yelled.

'For Christ's sake, I wasn't going to touch him,' she said

to her boyfriend, but Arvid didn't hear that and he sprinted off into the rushes and didn't stop until he came to a clearing and there he stood panting and pulling up long reeds from the ground, one by one, until his hands were full.

He couldn't see the couple any more, but he could see the creek, it ran past nearby, and suddenly a whole family of swans waddled out of the rushes and into the water, six splashes one after the other and the splashing didn't stop, but it sounded different now and Mogens came rowing along with a huge grin on his face.

'Did you see them?' he said.

'Sure,' Arvid said. 'He almost bit her ear off. Wild stuff.'

He clambered into the boat and Mogens said: 'What the hell are you talking about? I meant the swans. Swans don't have ears. Not as far as I know.'

'I guess they don't,' Arvid said, and sat down on the rear seat.

'You losing your marbles or what?'

'No.'

'Good.'

Mogens rowed on and they came to a bend in the creek and when they were past it, the rushes on one side were gone and a large field sloped down to the bank. A herd of cows was grazing a short distance from the water and behind them was a small, grey tumbledown hay barn, which could be handy if it started to rain.

26

Mogens steered towards the bank for this was a good place to go ashore and discover things. In the water there were lots of eel traps, they could see the labels flapping and Mogens leaned over the side and pulled one up, but it was empty and Arvid was glad because eels were as disgusting as snakes.

The boat struck land with a thud. Arvid stood up to jump over the side, and then he couldn't stop thinking about them and there was a bulge in his trunks, it was quite sudden, he gasped for breath and it showed because all he had on was a pair of thin red bathing trunks with no pockets.

'Shit.'

'What?' Mogens said.

'Nothing,' Arvid said, jumping quickly to be the first on land.

He lay down on his stomach in the grass and thought of something else, thought of mountain passes covered with heath and miles of pure air above them, and the smell of tar from telegraph poles when you rested your head against the cracked wood in the boiling sun, he thought of the Bay of Naples where he had never been, but it was bluer than blue and the most beautiful in the world, and he heard Mogens tie up the boat, come after him and lie down at his side. But Arvid was sleepy now, the sun was big and hot and it burned his back and it felt good, for when he lay like this on the ground he couldn't feel the wind. He took a blade of grass and chewed it, the juicy, slightly bitter taste burned his tongue as he watched the cows, which were lazy now, as he was, they were all lying down. The air flowed above their rounded backs while they chewed the grass like he did, he was an animal and had no wish to be anything else.

'Do you believe in God?' Mogens said.

'No, I don't,' Arvid said from afar, but it couldn't have been him talking because he couldn't feel his lips moving and a mist fell before his eyes even though it was a perfectly clear day.

'Nor me, I guess,' Mogens said. 'I'm not all that sure though,' but Arvid wasn't listening any more, he was sleeping and in his dream everything was warm and round and when he woke up Mogens was on his feet throwing clods of earth at the cows.

'Hey, why are you doing that?' Arvid said, and was wide awake and as clear as ice.

'It got so quiet here for a while,' Mogens said. 'Something's got to happen.' His voice was calm, but his right arm was firing off clods of earth with easy force.

'Goddamn it, stop doing that,' Arvid said, but Mogens didn't stop.

All the cows were standing now except for one, and Mogens took aim again and hit the cow's rump with the clod, and it didn't get up, it was suddenly standing. Arvid lay in the grass looking between its legs and said: 'Mogens.'

28

'Yes?'

'That last one wasn't a cow.'

'Not a cow? What do you mean?'

'It hasn't got udders.'

'Oh, shit,' Mogens said, and his arm fell in slow motion and a last clod fell to the ground and Arvid got up and sensed something in his chest, as if he were angry, but he wasn't.

'I'm off,' Mogens said, because the animal turned, and it was a bull, that was easy to see now. It scraped the ground with one hoof, harder and harder until the sandy soil formed a cloud around its legs. It started to move and at once Arvid felt he wasn't afraid, not at all and he tore off his red trunks and waved them in the air and the bull tossed its head.

'Are you crazy?' Mogens shouted from the boat. 'He'll tear your dick off!' But Arvid didn't answer, just waved his trunks even more eagerly as he shouted: '*Toro*! *Toro*!' and the bull moved faster and broke into a run. Arvid watched it coming closer and knew this was how it should be, there was no one who could get him, no one who could touch him, and a wind rose in his chest and blew, he could really hear it and he smiled.

'*Toro*! *Toro*! Come on, you bastard!' he yelled, and he was naked and invincible, he was Huckleberry Finn, he was Pelle the Conqueror, he was Arvid Jansen, and the bull was pounding towards him with lowered horns, but

Arvid didn't turn until he could see the whites of its eyes and then he turned slowly and stuck his bum out and then he ran. Not too fast, but fast enough and he was by the creek and threw himself in with a victorious laugh, swam a few strokes and got to the boat and pulled himself up.

He stood on the rear seat with his backside facing Mogens, who was rowing for dear life, he waved the red shorts in the air like a wet flag and felt the wind on his bare hips and chest as never before and he shouted: 'No one touches me! No one will ever knock me down! The bull stood with its front legs in the water and bellowed and Arvid laughed again.

'You're stark raving mad,' Mogens said, and Arvid heard his voice as if for the first time in ages and sat down and slowly the wind dropped until it wasn't blowing at all and he felt so empty and without air that he could barely breathe.

Mogens sent him a strange sidelong glance.

'Why don't you believe in God?' he said.

'What?'

'Why don't you believe in God?'

Arvid stared at the thick rushes with their brown tops and the dragonflies whirring like small helicopters in all the greenery and didn't feel like answering, but in the end he said: 'Because he killed my brother.'

'You haven't got a brother. Just a sister.'

'That's what I'm saying. But I did have one, for three

months. He was born early and was dying and I prayed to God to let him live, but he died anyway.'

'That wasn't God's fault!'

'Of course it was. He can fix everything, but he didn't give a shit.'

'But don't you think he *exists*?'

'Sure he exists, but he's got nothing to do with me. I can take care of myself.'

Mogens grinned. 'You're the craziest kid I know,' he said. 'I wish you were a girl. Only girls are as crazy as you and I've always liked those crazy girls. It'd be great if you were a girl.'

Arvid didn't have the strength to get angry.

'I'm not a damn girl,' was all he said.

BY HIS OWN HAND

He fell and fell and fell and made a grab for the dream, but it was gone before he landed on the floor beside the bed. And even though he knew the dream was bad, churning away in a corner of the room, he rolled over twice and stretched out his hands, took a deep breath and smiled. He saw the stripes of light on the ceiling move, the blinds rustled and he felt the morning air on his cheek from the open window. A cycle bell rang in the street and the sound mingled with the drone of his father's snoring.

Gry mumbled from the mattress, rolled over and said: 'Is that you, Arvid? Happy birthday, good night,' and rolled back.

Arvid grinned. '*Buona notte,*' he said. Gry wasn't like him, she was tired in the morning, on holidays too. He got up, stepped over her and tiptoed into the living room. Above the piano Jesus was sitting on the Mount of Olives with his chin in his hands staring sadly beyond Jerusalem, the moon was a pale glow, it was night for Jesus and would never be anything else, but for Arvid it was morning, with hot bread rolls and cocoa for breakfast, secret smiles from Gry and a parcel on the table. And day dawned and he was allowed to go to Grandfather's workshop because it was his birthday and he was twelve.

They walked up Danmarksgade, looking in the windows, taking their time, Grandfather first in his threadbare suit, without a tie, his hands on his hips, and Arvid two steps behind. Pennants flapped on long lines across the street, from building to building, flying the Danish and Norwegian and Swedish and German colours. Arvid pretended it was for his birthday even though he knew it was to welcome the tourists, and they turned into a gateway and on the other side of the yard was a small, half-timbered house with two doors. To the left there was a flat with rose bushes beneath the windows and to the right was the workshop. Arvid could smell the fresh chipboard long before Grandfather unlocked the door.

The room was long and narrow and at the end there were two dusty windows where the sun shone in on the bandsaw that was standing in the middle of the floor and was dangerous. The blade was shiny and honed and could send out howls that chilled you to the marrow. Arvid had always gone into the yard to wait there when Grandfather used the saw, but this year for the first time he stayed inside and watched without holding his ears and felt the howl run down his spine.

On the right-hand wall above the workbench tools were hanging on hooks with their outlines behind them to show where everything belonged. When Grandfather entered the workshop in the morning there were never any tools lying around, every hook held its hammer or plane or hacksaw from the previous evening and all the wood shavings had been swept into a pile beside the door. When the pile was big enough Grandfather filled two jute bags and put them in the front of the delivery bike and pedalled off to an old billiards friend, who used the shavings to light his wood-burner. Grandfather and Grandmother had an oil stove.

Everything was brown inside, light or dark in the sun and the shade, except the saw and knife blades, which were rust-free and glinting, and Grandfather took off his jacket and hung it on the peg behind the door and folded his shirtsleeves up to the elbows and put the large, brown apron on. Arvid didn't have a jacket, only upper-class kids wore one in the summer, so he took off his jumper and hung it beside his grandfather's jacket. He couldn't fold up his shirtsleeves because he had a T-shirt underneath, but Grandfather gave him a little apron that Grandmother had sewn especially for him.

He was given a big block of wood and a hammer and a chisel. On the wood Grandfather had drawn lines to show Arvid where he should chisel to turn the block into a boat. It was the same piece of wood and the same boat every year. Arvid wasn't all that interested, he wasn't much good at woodwork anyway, but it was handy to have something to do while he watched Grandfather working, and that was what he liked.

Grandfather could take a piece of wood in his hand, gently weigh it, fasten it in the vice and after a quarter of an hour it was something completely different. He tightened the vice around Arvid's block of wood and Arvid watched his hands working, he couldn't keep his eyes off them, for everything the hands did seemed so easy even though they were big and hard and gnarled, and when Grandfather clenched his fists the knuckles rose up like white mountain peaks. His skin was so tight Arvid was afraid it would split. Grandfather saw Arvid's eyes and held out his hands.

'Hit them. Come on, hit them as hard as you can!' This was an old game which was amusing only for Grandfather, but Arvid knew he had to do it, so he hit one of them.

'No, not like that, as *hard* as you can!' Arvid punched with his fist and it hurt so much he had to grit his teeth not to scream.

Without looking at Arvid, Grandfather took his fist away and said: 'Hands can do so much. They can make furniture for example, but what I regret is all the hens they have strangled. Far too many hens.'

Arvid imagined Grandfather's hands strangling hens, twisting their necks. Once he had gone to use the outdoor toilet at Aunt Kari and Uncle Alf's farm and when he opened the lid there was a hen's head down there, but the beak was still opening and closing, making sounds. He stayed away for several days afterwards.

Grandfather grew up on a farm. It wasn't a small farm, but there were so many of them they had to work round the clock to feed everyone. Great-grandfather would drive his children like animals, would harness them to the plough if he had to, and he grafted as hard himself, and when he finally became so fragile he didn't have the strength to carry on, he went to the barn and hanged himself from one of the beams. That was when Grandfather realised he wanted to be a cabinetmaker and left for town even though he was the one to inherit the farm, and when Arvid asked him questions about the old days he seldom got any answers.

His great-grandfather didn't have a proper grave, just a plaque on the ground by the gate to the cemetery. Arvid had seen it, he could just make out what it said: BY HIS OWN HAND.

'Why did you strangle hens, Granddad?' Arvid said, and Grandfather looked at him as if he were stupid and then he felt stupid and didn't like it.

Arvid chopped away at the block of wood and after two blows with the hammer he had already gone inside the line, he couldn't control the chisel and Grandfather eyed him with that puzzled expression he always had when Arvid was with him in the workshop. Arvid blushed and Grandfather kept on working. He had been to the butcher's the day before and got two big bones that he cut up and ground down to two small pieces, which in turn became shiny, elegant fittings for the keyholes in the dresser he was making. Grandfather worked fast and beautifully and Arvid stood watching with the chisel hanging from one hand and the hammer from the other, but gradually the stench from the honing of the bones was so strong that he put down the tools and apron and went towards the door. On the threshold he stood with one foot in and one foot out, and Grandfather laughed behind him.

'Smells of dead bodies, doesn't it?' he shouted through the noise of saw cutting bone, and Arvid walked across the yard into the street, where the sun was shining and cars drove much too fast in both directions. He didn't know what dead bodies smelled like and didn't want to know, and he strode along the pavement away from where Grandmother and Grandfather lived, towards the Løveapoteket and Kirkeplassen and the bus terminal and when he came to the big junction, he turned left towards the railway station.

Inside the station there were large posters with pictures of trains travelling all over the world, and he stopped in front of the one with the train to Hamburg, the locomotive with the stylish front and the carriages in a long line behind steaming over a bridge like the one over the Limfjord and he thought maybe he would like to be a train driver and sit at the front of a train and go wherever he wanted and feel the speed as he leaned out of the window as he had seen in a film at Grorud Cinema. But he knew he would never be a train driver, he had no idea what he wanted to be, except perhaps for one thing.

He went on to the platform where a train would soon be leaving for Ålborg. The steps up to the nearest carriage door were tempting, but he walked past and along the whole train to the end of the platform and down the little steps and walked along the gravel beside the rails and on for quite a long way.

The sleepers smelled of tar and in some places dandelions protruded between the small stones and there were bushes between the rails and the fence by the road. He crouched down behind one of them, for he knew he was trespassing. Then he heard the whistle and from a distance he watched the train leaving the station. Soon it had picked up a good speed and he waited until it was close and when the locomotive had passed he jumped up from behind the bush and stood by the rails and felt the draught from the carriages ruffle his hair. He held his feet together and his knees stiff and found his balance in the soles of his feet and then he leaned forward with a straight back while trying to breathe evenly. At first he kept his eyes closed and then he forced them open and he saw the flickering lights so close that it hurt, he felt the throbbing of the wheels on the rail joints shake his body and after the whole train had passed and he had survived he held his arms aloft, made a V-for-victory sign and whirled round twice. Then he ran his fingers through his hair and rubbed his face and there was blood on one hand from a cut to his cheek and he didn't know when he got that, but it didn't matter because he *had* survived.

He clambered over the fence and was on the road that ran along the park, and he knew the way from there. It was a long walk, but he kept up a good pace and was home well in time for lunch at twelve. They were having meatballs, which he always chose when it was his birthday.

Grandfather came home to eat and Arvid was sitting on the divan in the living room when he returned. Grandfather looked at him and was about to say something, and Arvid could already hear the snap of the words even before he had opened his mouth, but then Grandfather changed his mind and only winked as if they were sharing a secret. Arvid sighed with relief although he had no idea what the secret might have been.

TANGO, IN A FLAT,
BROAD-BRIMMED HAT

It was the quiet hour after lunch. Arvid sat reading at the bottom of the steps by the door that stood open to the yard. The sun was shining and the pattern of the bars in the gate fell on to the tarmac and he could hear bikes trundling past in the street and people calling to each other in Danish and every now and then a car. It was so still by the steps that he heard the flies in the little window. The door to the milk shop was ajar, he was keeping watch and when the bell rang and someone came in, he was supposed to shout to his grandmother that there was a customer. She was up in the living room playing the piano. It had a strange sound, it was an old cinema piano that Grandfather had bought cheap and remade and when Grandmother played, it always sounded like a silent movie.

He was reading a book called *His Brother's Keeper*. It was a Christian book and he didn't like Christian books, but there was nothing else here apart from *Pelle the Conqueror*, and he had read that twice. The book had been printed in Gothic script. He was learning to read Gothic script because he knew there were so many books that had been published in this script and he had to read them before they rotted and were gone and no one would know what people used to think in the old days. But he was a bit fed up with them always thinking Christian thoughts.

Grandmother sang psalms, always psalms, and she had written them herself and composed the music, she was a writer of psalms and had four notebooks full of them. He knew many people had told her to send them in to get them published in a book, but she didn't want to, for it would be like making yourself important at the expense of God, and that was pride, and pride came before a fall.

Her voice was high-pitched and different from when she spoke. She always spoke in a low voice, at least when Grandfather was in the room, but now it was high-pitched and shrill. There was something disgusting about this voice and yet there was an allure that tugged and tugged at him and wanted all of him, but he knew that if he let himself go he would be swallowed up and then there was no knowing what would happen.

Fortunately the bell rang and a customer came in, and Arvid dropped *His Brother's Keeper* and called for Grandmother and then the quiet hour was over. Everyone appeared from their secret places, where they had been resting, and Søren stood in the yard, Mogens' father, waiting beside his car. It was still Arvid's birthday and Grandfather had taken the rest of the day off to go for a drive. Grandmother had to look after the shop and Arvid's father had to go out to do some negotiating, and only he and maybe Arvid's mother knew what it was about, but the others got into the Opel Kapitän, with Søren sitting in the driver's seat.

They drove down Danmarksgade and along Søndergade, where Aunt Else lived, heading south. At Møllehuset, with the bandstand and the little river and the small bridges and the swans, they turned right up a hill and then they were in the woods and carried on up. It was nice to be in a car, Arvid rarely was, just the taxi home from the ship a few times and on the back of the 'Blåmann', Sveen's lorry at their house back home in Norway. Sveen worked at a toy factory and his cellar was full of them, because he had these light fingers and drank so much it was a mystery he still had a driving licence.

The forest wasn't big, but it was dense and a little gloomy as the trees weren't spruces like at home, but oak and beech, and the crowns met high up and made a ceiling. Everything was dim and mysterious and the few places where the sun burst through it were so bright they couldn't see a thing.

They drove past the café in the clearing, where Arvid thought they were going to stop and eat a hot Danish pastry, but they didn't.

'Look there, Arvid,' his mother said, pointing, 'under the big tree.' Under an oak tree two deer stood, chewing and staring at them with almond eyes as the car rumbled past. They didn't stir, just stood with their heads held high and their ears pricked and Arvid said: 'In Denmark we go through a little wood and we see deer, while at home in the Lillomarka forest we go for mile upon mile, Sunday after Sunday, and don't see so much as a fox. There isn't even a single spruce tree here.'

'They aren't wild, you know,' Gry said. 'The forest ranger keeps an eye on them and feeds them. They eat from his hand if they're hungry enough.'

'Makes no difference. A deer's a deer. I've never seen deer before.'

He turned and saw them through the rear window, they were standing in the same place and were beautiful and slim and could surely run as fast as lightning if they wanted. One of them slowly turned its head with the big antlers and watched the car leaving, and its long horns were grey against the greenery behind, and Arvid just had to swallow.

Then they suddenly turned out of the forest, and past the tall tower you could see from miles away when you came in from the sea, and on to the road that took them over the ridge facing south, and everywhere there was light and air. The road wound its way along the ridge's back and to the left the sea was almost standing upright. It was so blue it seemed as though the colour was not a real colour at all, and on the horizon the island of Læsø was balancing. He had never seen that far.

'Can we stop?' he said, and Søren pulled in because it was Arvid's birthday, and Arvid opened the door and jumped out on to the verge and walked a few metres down the slope and lay in the grass. It was so steep it was almost like standing, he could rest his body and at the same time see as far as he wanted. He took deep breaths again and again, and there was air enough for a lifetime and he promised himself he would never start smoking. His mother could never inhale as much air into her lungs as he could. His chest was a balloon that couldn't burst, it just filled up and sent blue air to all corners of his body and his body turned into something so light and delicate he could jump off the nearest cliff and fly like Peter Pan.

Afterwards it felt narrow and clammy in the car. They drove on into the country and down from the ridge and they came to a place with a few farms huddled together surrounded by vast fields. One of them was Grandfather's farm and they stopped there and Grandfather got out of the car, walked to the gate and stood there looking. The farmhouse was freshly painted and what had once been the midden was filled with rocks now and in the cracks flowers had been planted. It looked nice and Grandfather stood stock-still without saying anything, no one said anything. Arvid gazed out over the fields and tried to imagine Grandfather before the plough with his father at his back holding a whip, but it was not possible, for Grandfather was only Grandfather the way he was now, with a bent back and a moustache and not like he must have been then. Grandfather got back into the car still not saying anything, and they drove on, along an empty road. Then his mother made faces and squirmed on the seat beside Arvid and finally she said: 'I think we'll have to stop again.'

'What?' Søren said.

'Needs must!'

'Oh,' he said, but it was bare here, there was not a bush to crouch behind, not a fence, and he scratched his head and looked around.

'You'll have to go behind the car,' he said. 'Everyone look straight ahead.'

His mother got out and went behind the car and squatted down. They waited for a while and suddenly Søren grinned and winked at Grandfather. He put the car in gear and they set off.

'No!' Arvid said, and Gry said: 'Stop, you idiot,' in a voice so sharp it didn't sound like hers at all, but Grandfather laughed and Søren laughed and drove on a way before he stopped the car. Arvid looked out of the rear window and there was his mother squatting in the distance and then she got up and started to run, faster and faster, and now Arvid could see her contorted face, and she caught up with them and raised her arm and banged the boot with her fist. She banged her way around, so hard there were bound to be dents in the coachwork.

She wrenched open the door on Grandfather's side, grabbed his jacket and said in a low voice: 'That's the last time you leave me in the lurch! Absolutely the last! You watch it or you won't see your grandchildren for years!' and she slammed the door and Arvid wondered why she had taken out her anger on Grandfather.

Grandfather sat like a statue on the front seat, as if the stone he was made of would shatter if he so much as moved a finger, and Søren stared through the window, hands in his lap. His mother got on to the back seat, next to Arvid, and there was total silence until Gry could stand it no longer and had to cough and then his mother said: 'Drive!'

Søren slowly shook his head, but he raised his hands and finally the car moved off.

There were the farms again, and a cluster of spruce trees, as small as toys, Friesian cows and then mustard fields so yellow the light seemed to come up from the ground, not down from the sky, and on a hill stood the church where Great-grandfather's plaque was. The church was pretty with its white plastered walls and red-tiled roof, but no one dared ask Søren to stop. When the hill was behind them his mother began to sing in a voice that was dark and not like Grandmother's, for his mother's voice was suddenly full of laughter, and she sang: '*Come prima più di prima t'amerò / Per la vita, la mia vita ti darò / Sembra un sogno rivederti accarezzarti / Le tue mani fra le mani stringere ancor,*' all the way through the song and when she started a second time around Arvid joined in. His mother had taught him the song several years ago, he didn't understand a word, for the text was Italian, but he could sing it anyway and the words had a sound to them that he liked.

'Oh, my God!' Gry said, and started to laugh and Arvid laughed and Søren laughed wildly, he banged the wheel with both hands, making the car swerve in the road, and howled as if he had some kind of illness. The only person who wasn't laughing was Grandfather, but he was moving at least, he kept chewing his moustache and the car turned off the road and now they were in Sæby forest and that was their destination.

In a clearing stood a former hunting manor, but now it was a restaurant and had been one for a long time and the road they came on was narrow, bushes scraped against the car doors, but there was plenty of room to park in front of the main entrance.

They sat down by one of the big windows. The dust looked dense in the sunlight, but it didn't catch in your throat, which was strange, and there were pheasants on the grass outside. Søren walked across the chequered carpet into the kitchen to tell them they had arrived.

There was no one else in the room and it was so quiet that when they spoke it was still quiet. They sat as if inside a bubble and talked about what they would eat and that

47

was hot apple crumble with ice cream. When the woman came with the crumble and hot chocolate Arvid thought he had never tasted anything so good and never would again.

Afterwards they went outside and looked at the forest and the pheasants, but there was something about the day that had ended, no one could think of anything more to do or say and Søren walked nervously around the car to see if there were any scratches from the bushes, but what he found were small dents from Arvid's mother's fists and he touched them and said nothing.

Grandfather stood in front of the old manor house, hands in his pockets and his threadbare suit shining where his crooked back had chafed, and then he raised one hand and stroked the length of his moustache with his index finger. He came over and stood by Arvid and put one hand on his shoulder. Arvid's shoulder twitched, but he didn't move away and Grandfather said: 'Do you know when I was last here, Arvid?'

'No.'

'More than forty years ago. A friend and I came here to dance the tango. This place was a dance hall then and the only one on the coast where they played the tango. Mostly soldiers came here from their barracks, but we too wanted to come here, so we got dressed up and set off. That is, we walked. It was a long way, you know that now.'

Arvid had seen pictures in *Norsk Ukeblad* magazine of

men in black hats and tight trousers, and women with flowers in their hair and dresses that were tight across the bum and wide at the bottom, dancing the tango.

'Was it fun?'

'We never got that far. At the entrance we were stopped by a breathless soldier who said we should turn and go back home at once. He had lost his fine cap, I remember. There was a police raid going on, he said.'

'Why was that? Were they drinking moonshine?'

Grandfather laughed. 'No, it was the tango, it was forbidden. Then I married your grandmother and that was it. I haven't been here since. Until today.'

Arvid looked up at his grandfather, who was stroking his moustache again, and then his mother called, it was time to go, enough was enough.

That night Grandfather danced the tango in a flat, broad-brimmed hat in a large dance hall with chandeliers hanging from the ceiling and a pheasant pattern on the floor. His moustache was sharp as a dagger, it had a matt gleam in the light and the shadows covered the rest of his face and when Arvid woke up and remembered the dream, Grandfather was never quite the same again.

YOU KNOW I DON'T DRINK

Grandmother and his mother were in the kitchen peeling potatoes. It was plaice for lunch, and not for the first time this summer. The kitchen was too narrow for more than one person, and through the half-open door Arvid could see how his mother drew back her shoulders and moved away, and now and again, with a flick of her hand, she removed a lock of hair from her forehead. Grandmother started crying, and not for the first time this summer.

Arvid sat in a chair by the living-room window reading the book Gry had given him for his birthday. It was called *20,000 Leagues Under the Sea* and was written by Jules Verne. It was raining in Lodsgade, it was still morning, though dark as if it were evening, water streaming down the window-panes, and Captain Nemo standing on the little deck of the *Nautilus* with his arms crossed, watching with steely eyes an English warship sink. Arvid felt a chill down his spine, it was something so terrible and wonderful that he couldn't sit still, he jumped up from the chair and went over to his mother to tell her about it. But she was on her way out of the kitchen with the potato peeler in her hand, and it stuck out like a knife, and Arvid leaped to the side. She looked down and when she saw what she was holding, she threw it to the floor and said: 'I have to go out for a walk.'

'It's raining outside,' Arvid said.

'All the better,' she said, making for the wardrobe.

'I want to go with you.'

'No!'

'Yes. I want to go with you,' he said. 'I'm twelve years old. I can go with you now!' She sent him a look he didn't like, but then she gave a little laugh.

'All right, you can come along, but stay behind me, is that understood?'

'Sure,' he said, and glanced into the living room where Gry was watching them and she wanted to come too, but he had asked first and now it was too late for her. He opened his palms, as if to say sorry, but she turned to the wall.

His father came up the steps from the backyard and he looked at them in surprise. 'Where are you going?'

'Out!'

'But why? It's raining and soon it will be lunch-time.'

'I walk where I want, all right?' his mother said, and Arvid waited, but his father didn't know what to say, and Arvid bent down and put on his boots.

They put their raincoats on and under her chin his mother tied the kerchief that she wore when she couldn't care less what she looked like, and they went down the steps and into the street. It was still raining as they walked down Lodsgade and it got worse when they came to the harbour and along the quays, and there was a wind too, the waves beat against the mole and Arvid realised he should have had his sou'wester on, and he turned his head to avoid the rain blowing straight into his face.

'Are you sure you want to come with me? We're still not far from home.'

He just walked on a bit faster without answering, and his mother shrugged. 'Have it your way,' she said.

The shipyard cranes swung round on themselves and disappeared into the grey rain above, so tall were they, and lightning flashed in the sky, a welding flame flashed from inside a rusty boat and a clap of thunder boomed. They had reached the fishing harbour, the blue-painted boats rocked and bumped against the timber structure of the quays. Many of them had come in from the sea to dock because of the weather, and there was a smell of fish from the boats and fishmeal from a nearby building, of wet ropes, of wet dust on the ground, and tar. Arvid looked around him and imagined he was in a film, in *Salka Valka*, which his mother liked so much, with Margaretha Krook and her little daughter walking in the rain from house to house knocking on doors, but no one would take them in, not even the Salvation

Army, and then they were at the foot of the mole and his mother began to walk out along the narrow footpath.

'Is this where you're going?' Arvid called.

His mother nodded.

'But it's dangerous. You could be blown into the sea!'

'Ha! I've walked here ever since I was a little girl, and I walked here when I was expecting Gry,' his mother said, and walked on.

'You don't *have* to come with me,' she said into the wind.

'But I do,' Arvid said, though only he could hear that.

The wind was coming off the sea, but a timber windbreak had been built along most of the mole and when he lowered his head it wasn't so bad, for he was small, but the rain beat against his mother's head and shoulders and she crouched and drew the kerchief tighter around her face.

He stayed close to her back and they walked quite a distance, almost the whole way out to the little grey lighthouse by the harbour entrance. The wind kept coming and every now and again she stared up into the air and then wiped her face, for it was soaking wet, and not once did she look at Arvid and so he didn't dare talk to her. Again there was thunder and lightning and she turned and said: 'The weather was just like this when your sister was born. I was in bed looking through the window. One window was open and the rain was coming in. No one had thought to close it.'

'At Aker Hospital at home?'

'No, on a little island south of here.'

'Wasn't Gry born in Norway?'

'No.'

'Couldn't Dad have closed the window?' He turned his back to the wind so she could hear what he was saying.

'He wasn't there.'

'Grandmother or Grandfather then?'

'They weren't there either.'

'Why not?'

'Because, as they saw it, I had stumbled from the path.' She laughed drily. 'Jesus!'

He held on to the windbreak and looked out over the sea. It was a leaden grey and the waves rolled towards him with their white crests and thundered against the big rocks by the shoreline and the spray was taller than him.

'What are you thinking about,' she said in his ear and he considered what he was thinking about and it was still the same.

'About *Salka Valka*.'

She gazed at him in surprise. 'The film?'

'Yes.'

'The opening?'

He nodded and ran a hand over his wet face.

'Me too,' she said. 'Just now.'

He didn't think that was so strange and perhaps she didn't either and they were standing by the little lighthouse now, it was the middle of the day, but so dark the light was on. A lamp turned inside sending flashes out into the stormy weather and he started to cry and the light was orange and it went round and round and he was crying and he didn't know why.

He cried and felt his chest grow big and then contract to almost nothing, he gasped for breath, clenched his fists and she held his shoulder with one hand and his chin with the other and turned his head round to look into his face. He shoved her away roughly.

'Don't you touch me! I'm twelve years old. I can take care of myself!' He turned on his heel and began to run back and she followed him at a more sedate pace.

'Hey, you, boy. You're supposed to be behind me, don't you remember?' she shouted and then he stopped and waited until she had passed him and he walked behind her, a few steps from her back now, until they were in the harbour again.

On their way up Lodsgade she suddenly stopped and went into the Ferry Inn. He glanced up the street at the dairy shop and followed her in.

The room was empty except for a woman who was playing a one-arm bandit in the corner and the landlord behind the bar. They sat down at a window table.

'Shouldn't we go home for lunch now?'

'They can have their plaice,' she said. 'I'm sick of fish. What would you like?'

'Rissoles.'

He turned and watched the woman in the corner mechanically pulling the lever of the one-arm bandit. It was such a regular sound that after a while he wasn't certain who was pulling what. She had a cigarette poked between her lips and it was almost burned down to the filter, ash hung off in a long arc, the cigarette kept burning, neither her face nor her mouth moved and he stared at her, wouldn't it fall off soon? But it didn't, and then she hit the jackpot. The bowl jingled and rattled and she released the lever and reached down with her hand to collect the money and then the ash spread over her blouse like an avalanche, he was sure there would soon be a boom, but everything was very quiet and she didn't notice.

The landlord came with two rissoles, a Jolly Cola and a beer on a tray. He was a big man with a leather apron covered in sticky brown stains and he spilled some of the beer on the tablecloth when he put it down.

'But you don't drink beer.'

'Today I do.' She smiled. 'Don't worry. I won't turn into an alcoholic because of one beer.'

He didn't think she would, but he didn't like her drinking beer. He had never seen her drink beer. She took a large swig and obviously enjoyed it and he looked down at the rissoles and began to tuck in.

She didn't drink, but not everyone knew that. At home in Veitvet most people had a drink now and then, and once when they were sitting on the steps outside having coffee in the afternoon and his father came home from work, she did something unusual. She stood up and wrapped her arms around Dad's neck and gave him a hug, for it was pay day and they were short of money. The next day their neighbour, fru Bomann, came over and said with a smarmy smile: 'Well, fru Jansen, you were a bit drunk yesterday, weren't you? We all are once in a while.'

'But you know I don't drink,' his mother said.

'Oh, don't give me that. I saw you hugging your husband on the steps,' fru Bomann said, and Arvid too thought it a bit strange because not once had he seen anyone from their terraced house give each other a hug.

The window was filthy. He took a napkin and wiped it and looked into the street. The rain was hammering down and the wind was making Lodsgade look like the rapids in a river and then all of a sudden it stopped and everything turned oddly quiet. He held his breath and looked at his mother. She was gazing out of the window with a smile that had nothing to do with him, and the sun was shining now, steam rising from the black tarmac, they could hear the harbour train clanking past on its way to the station, sirens howled at the shipyard for lunch and the first blue-clad cyclists passed the window and it was twelve o'clock.

'Mum?'

'Yes?'

'That German, is it true they never found him?'

'Which German?'

'The one who was caught in a riptide and pulled down to the bottom after the War.'

'Oh him. No, they never found him. Why do you ask?'

'Because I dream about him at night. It's scary.'

She reached her hand across the table and tousled his wet fringe and made it into an Elvis quiff. He let her do it.

'I used to dream about him too,' she said. 'One winter when it seemed as if the ice had covered the whole sea I skated out to the lighthouse island with a friend. When I got home I was grounded even though I was an adult. Your grandfather was furious and he really had a temper in those days. A boy had fallen through the ice the day before and drowned, but I hadn't heard about it. That night I dreamed it was me who fell through and sank into the cold, green water, right to the bottom, and there I saw the German.'

'What did he look like?'

'He was standing on the seabed, wearing a uniform and helmet, saying "Heil Hitler."'

'You couldn't hear that underwater, could you?'

'No, but there were bubbles coming out of his mouth and the bubbles said "Heil Hitler." I could see it.'

He was not so sure about that, the accident had happened *after* the War, but it was only a dream and now they shared a dream, even if the dream was a nightmare.

'I'll never forget that dream,' she said. 'Eat up your food now.'

FORGET IT, ARVID SAID

When he awoke in the middle of the night in his room at home in Veitvet and the window was open and it was summer, he could hear the music from Alnabru shunting station. There was a sound of singing drifting through the night and he knew what it was that made it. During the day he had stood in the field below Linderud Farm and had seen the goods trains trundling down from the Donkey's Back into one of the many tracks that ran along-side each other at the bottom of the Grorud Valley. It was the wheels that made the sound, although in the day you never heard them, and *that* gave you an eerie feeling, for you never saw any people there, just the wagons rolling down, nothing pulling them, several at a time all on their own rails.

But at night the sounds were clear, like a chorus of notes and he didn't have to get out of bed to know the sky was lit up above Alnabru, yellow and red and orange that gave the music colour. Sometimes he got up anyway when he couldn't sleep. Then he leaned on the window-sill thinking he would like to work there when he grew up or on one of the trains that passed by and see the lights close up and feel the excitement of them at night. But he was twelve years old and he knew that life was already heading somewhere else.

When he woke up in the room above the dairy shop and the window was open it took him time to realise that the music from the railway wagons wasn't there, and when he did, he was wide awake.

Lying in bed between his mother and father was too hot, he couldn't sleep like that any more, it was ridiculous, he had to get up. The alarm clock by the bedhead showed half-past two, but never mind, he couldn't sleep. He wriggled out of bed, dressed and went into the living room. There wasn't enough space here, Grandfather was snoring on the divan, so he went out past the kitchen and down the stairs. The dairy shop door was open. He could hear Grandmother talking to herself or to God in the Aquarium. The key was in the yard door and he opened it and went out. He stood still on the tarmac and could feel it was a little too cold for just a T-shirt, so he went back in, up the stairs, fetched a sweater, and when he went outside again he was fine. The sky was overcast, but it was dry and the grey weather and semi-gloom made the air seem as if it were filled with thin smoke, smoke you couldn't see but knew was there.

There was a bike stand against one wall of the outside toilet, which wasn't a proper outside toilet because it had a flush, and he went over and climbed on to the bike stand

and stretched up and, once he had a good grip of the edge of the roof, he pulled himself up.

He lay on the roof looking into the air, it was three o'clock in the morning and in his mouth he had one of his mother's cigarettes. He didn't light it, he didn't even have any matches and he had no wish to smoke either, it just felt right to have it there. There was a smell of menthol tobacco and roofing felt and the faint perfume of roses from the toilet wall and several other smells he couldn't name. They came from the street and down from the harbour and from the fields to the west of town.

You could breathe here, he drew the air deep down into his lungs and slowly released it and heard the rush in his ears. He lay quite still and heard another rush and it was the sea. In the far distance he heard a dog barking and suddenly it howled and then went quiet.

On a house on the other side of the backyard there was a big picture advertising Tuborg beer. It was hard to read through the smoky air, but he knew what it said and the man in the picture seemed more alive now than during the day. Mogens lived in that house. His window faced the yard and Arvid picked up a little stone from the roof, stood up, and sent the stone flying, and he was good at it, the stone hit the target and Arvid was startled by the loud, sharp crack on the window-pane. He didn't dare try again and when no one opened up he lay back down. He closed his eyes and thought he was finally tired enough to sleep, but then he heard a voice, saying: 'What the hell! Is that you there?'

He opened his eyes and Mogens was standing in the window and he was naked from the waist up and his hair was dishevelled.

'Yep,' Arvid said.

'A bit crowded indoors?' Mogens said, and his voice was loud between the houses and Arvid didn't like it. He didn't answer and Mogens rubbed his eyes and scratched his head and dropped his hands, probably to scratch his crotch.

'Shall we go fishing?' he said.

'Now?' Arvid said. 'Where?'

'From the mole. It's good there. I can't sleep any more anyway.' Arvid gave the idea some thought, the wind wasn't blowing now, everywhere it was still, everything was quite different, so he said: 'Yes, OK, but I don't feel like going back in.'

'That's all right. I've got two rods,' Mogens said. 'Hang on a moment and I'll be with you.'

Arvid lay on the roof waiting with the cigarette bobbing up and down between his lips until Mogens came and banged the fishing rods on the roof, and then he crawled over the edge and eased himself down. Mogens had an extra windcheater too and Arvid put it on.

'It's not *that* warm out,' said Mogens, who had remembered the key to the metal gate, and he unlocked it and it creaked and swung open and they walked down Lodsgade. There wasn't a soul around, only the empty street and a cat that shot round the corner of a house, but cats don't have souls.

'Do you want me to light that?' Mogens said, taking a match from his pocket. Arvid felt his lips and the cigarette was still there.

'No,' he said, and took it out of his mouth and put it into the windcheater pocket.

It was slowly getting lighter, but the smoke held and softened the air, and made all the brick walls seem soft as well. He slid his hand around the corner of a house and was surprised when something felt hard against his palm.

'Shit,' said Mogens, 'I forgot the bait. We've got to have some bait.'

'What kind of bait?'

'Lugworms. That's the best, that's what fish like best.'

'Where are we going to get hold of that now?'

Mogens turned and went back and Arvid followed him. They went up Danmarksgade and started to walk north. The street was empty and strange here too, apart from a man who was walking ahead of them and singing: '*I'm an oat plant, of bells I am made. More than twenty, I think, on every blade.*' He was drunk, his body was made of soft rubber, but his singing was good and it was a sad song to listen to in an empty street at night. He didn't hit a wrong note, but he needed the whole pavement to move forward.

'His name's Mortensen,' Mogens said. 'He used to work at the shipyard as a turner, but then he got divorced, went nuts and now he drinks all the time.'

Mogens crossed the street. Arvid watched Mortensen, who slowly became smaller and smaller until he turned a corner and vanished. He couldn't quite cope with the bend and had to step into the street. Arvid didn't know anyone who was divorced, it must have been hell. You got divorced and went crazy and then you began to drink. That's how it was.

He crossed the street after Mogens, who had stopped in front of a sports shop. Beside the display window was a machine, identical to the one that the baker's had. There were lots of small windows, one on top of the other, and if you inserted two 25-øre coins you could open one of the windows and behind it was a coconut slice or a butter cookie or a cinnamon biscuit or some other delicacy. But there were no cakes here. Behind every window was a paper cup, and in the cup were maggots, lugworms, that people had dug up on the beach after high tide and sold to the sports shop. Mogens put in four 25-øre coins and opened two of the windows and took the cups out. He gave one to Arvid.

'That should do us for now,' he said. 'Just empty the cup into your jacket pocket. I've had worms in there before.'

It was disgusting to walk with worms in your pocket, but he did as Mogens said. It came to mind too late that he had poured the mess over his cigarette that he had planned to put back in the Cooly packet.

They took a different way to the harbour from the one Arvid was used to. They came from the north this time, from Gammeltorv and the courthouse and the gaol, and they went down by Admiral Tordenskjold's house. Tordenskjold had lived there once, they claimed, and on a sign in black, peeling letters under one gable it said TORDENSKJOLD HOUSE. Arvid didn't think that was proof enough, for the house was an old shack and he couldn't picture Tordenskjold with his three-cornered hat and long curls and smart stick coming out of that splintered brown door. Tordenskjold was Norwegian, but there was a picture of him on all Danish matchboxes. If he had lived in this house he would have taken better care of it.

There were many old houses here with crooked roofs, but a fresh coat of paint made them look nice in yellow with black timbers, and the road was made of ancient cobblestones, which were hard to walk on without tripping, and between the houses you could see through to a long, brown beach where seaweed lay in great piles like birds' nests.

Arvid pointed and said: 'That's where Terje Vigen came ashore.'

'Who?'

'Terje Vigen,' Arvid said.

'Who the hell is he?'

'Was,' Arvid said. 'Don't you know who Terje Vigen was?'

The book was on a shelf at home between Helge Ingstad's *Trapper Life* and Maxim Gorky's *My Childhood*. It was his father's bookcase from before the War, but Arvid had never seen him reading any of the books in it. In the evening his father usually sat in a chair and dozed off with a Morgan Kane or Walt Slade Western in his lap. His hands were so big that the small, trashy books nearly vanished, and when they fell to the floor Arvid would say: 'You dropped your book.'

'What?'

'You fell asleep.'

'I did *not*.'

But he had and Arvid looked over at the bookcase and knew they couldn't talk about what was there, the conversation would be over before it even started, and he had to travel alone.

He did travel alone and he went wherever he wanted: he skied across Greenland, sailed on the *Gjøa* through the North-west Passage, stood two years before the mast in the storms around Cape Horn, saw the English pounding away at the fortifications around Sevastopol with bullets whizzing round their heads and the young count who was still not famous shouted: Get under cover, you young fool! He lay in the grass on the banks of the Mississippi and saw Huck Finn get on board the raft with the fish they were going to fry on the fire, and with Martin Eden he walked into the bourgeois houses of San Francisco afraid his broad shoulders would knock all the porcelain over when he turned round, and he didn't even know how to eat with a knife and fork like they did but decided he would learn everything that they knew and more. And he rowed with Terje Vigen from Norway to Denmark because his wife and children were starving and he made land right here, with aching hands and fingers that couldn't be straightened after all those freezing hours grasping the oars. He must have been so exhausted, and his back stiff as a board, but pleased too as he rowed back with what he came for. And then he strayed into the English blockade and everything was lost.

'Who was he then?'

'Who?'

'Terje Vigen!'

'Forget it,' Arvid said.

The island lay to the north and was barely visible, morning hadn't broken there yet, and was shrouded in mist, but it was lighter on the footpath and that was because they were here and not there. Halfway along the mole they climbed over the windbreak and jumped from one boulder to the next down to the water. These rocks were bigger than any he had seen in Denmark and he wondered how they had ended up here. His father said they had come with the ice from Norway in the Ice Age and that the whole of Denmark had in fact been left behind by Norway when the ice withdrew and that was a good thing for otherwise the Oslo Fjord wouldn't be there. But that didn't explain why the rocks were so neatly lined up along the mole.

Mogens assembled the rods and saw to the lines and reels and gave one to Arvid. When Arvid and his father went fishing at home in the Bunne Fjord they always fished from the shore using lures or jigged from a boat using mussels as bait on the many hooks hanging one above the other, but Mogens only used one hook with a lugworm. They cast the line with a lead weight and a float beyond the seaweed that was bobbing up and down in the shallow water, and the red and white float settled on the waves and floated as it was meant to. Then they slowly drew in the line and jerked up the hook before it got snagged in the seaweed and cast out again, leaving the hook in peace for a while before they reeled in again.

Mogens took hold of Arvid's arm and tried to help him as he was about to cast, but Arvid shook off his hand and said: 'I can do this on my own,' but he couldn't. The first

69

two attempts the hook got caught in the seaweed and he had to kneel down to untangle it and the sleeve of his jacket got soaked through. Gradually though he got the knack of it.

'What kind of fish are we after?' Arvid said.

'Flatfish,' Mogens said. 'Plaice.'

'Oh, no, not plaice!'

'You're not the only one who's sick of plaice,' Mogens said. 'Everyone in this town is sick of plaice. But it's different when you catch them yourself.'

'I hope so,' Arvid said.

His cast this time was perfect, the line flew through the air and the float landed well out. It was just a fluke, but Mogens smiled and gave a nod and after that they stood for a good while casting and reeling in, and as they fished the sun rose. He could feel its warmth straight away, it hit him in the face and chest and he decided that from now on everything would turn out fine. He tested himself, and thought about Mortensen really hard to see if it made him sad, but Mortensen was almost gone, the gloom in the streets was hard to imagine now, everywhere there was light and water, and beyond the water lay Sweden, but he couldn't see Sweden and he didn't want to either.

'How old is your sister, anyway?' Mogens asked.

'Almost fourteen.'

'She looks older,' Mogens said, but Arvid knew nothing about that, he only knew that Mogens seemed older than thirteen and a half, especially now, wearing his wind-cheater with the sun on his face and his hair swept back and his adult grip on the rod as he hauled in the fish. He had caught three plaice and sent them into the ever after with a sharp knife. Arvid hadn't caught anything, but for now it didn't matter.

'Gry,' Mogens said.

'What?'

'Nothing,' Mogens said, and Arvid didn't look at him, for now he felt such a powerful pull on the line that he almost lost his balance. The rod bent double and the winder jumped out of his hand and the line sang as it unwound.

'Christ, I've got a whopper here,' he shouted, trying to brake the reel, but the handle smashed against his thumb and he yelled: 'Goddamn it!'

Mogens jammed his rod between two rocks and sprinted over to Arvid, yanked the rod out of his hands and used the sleeve of his jacket as a brake to get the reel under control and slowly began to draw in the line.

'Hey, that's my fish,' Arvid hollered. 'Give me the rod.'

'Just wait a little,' Mogens said, still reeling in, and they saw a flash in the water, and what was out there was not a plaice.

'I think it's a cod,' Mogens said, 'a big one.'

'I don't give a shit if it's a cod or a shark, so long as it's not a plaice,' Arvid said. 'Give me my rod!'

'Actually it's my rod, but you can have it now,' Mogens said, although he didn't show the slightest sign of handing it over, he just stood there with his tongue sticking out one side of his mouth and a childish look on his face, and Arvid shouted: 'What the hell are you interested in my sister for anyway, you're only thirteen!'

He turned and leaped from rock to rock in a zigzag down to the water and he jumped in. It was deeper than he expected, it reached up to his chest and for a moment he couldn't catch his breath. He waited until his lungs were filled up again and he shouted to the shore: 'Cod is a Norwegian fish, you stick to your Danish plaice, *capiche*!' He grabbed the line and as Mogens reeled in, Arvid let it glide through his hands until he saw the fish in front of him. Then he stopped the line and held it tight. He lunged for the cod with his other hand and it thrashed its tail and was slippery in his wet fingers and every time he had a hold it shot out. But he could feel how alive it was, how its whole body was one writhing muscle. He had never held a fish in this way before and it was up at the surface now and he made another grab for it and the tail lashed against the palm of his hand and the water splashed into his face. He wasn't aware that his mouth was wide open, but now he could taste the saltwater and on the mole Mogens burst into laughter and Arvid coughed and lost his temper.

'Fucking cod!' he muttered, and drew his hands up into

the over-long jacket sleeves and used them as mittens to clamp the fish's tail in a tight grip, and pulled the fish through the seaweed and then out of the water with all the strength he had and smashed it against the nearest boulder and then it was still and Mogens wasn't laughing any more.

They stood on the path without moving. Water was streaming down Arvid's clothes, they could hear it dripping down on to the flagstones where they formed dark patches around his legs. The sun was up, but still it wasn't very warm.

'Are you cold?' Mogens said, and carefully squeezed Arvid's upper arm and was grown up again.

'No,' Arvid said, trying to keep his teeth from chattering.

'We'd better get the hell back home, or else you'll be ill,' Mogens said. He took two plastic bags from his jacket and put the three plaice in one and the cod in the other and gave it to Arvid. 'Here, take this. You've earned it. That kind of fishing I've only seen in the cinema.' He gave a wry smile. 'Come on and get yourself home.'

Arvid took the bag, opened it and looked down at the cod. It looked miserable. Its head was smashed, one eye was gone and he couldn't remember why he had done what he'd done. He felt a little sick.

'Shall we swap?' he said. 'My cod is as big as your three plaice.'

Mogens stood there. 'All right,' he said. 'But then you must promise to *run* home, is that clear?'

'It's clear,' Arvid said, and they exchanged bags and set off down the path at a jog, Arvid in front, his clothes steaming and there were sounds coming from his shoes he would've preferred not to hear, and then Mogens at his back and whenever Arvid slackened his pace, Mogens gave a shout to keep him going.

He ran until he reached Lodsgade and there he almost came to a halt and let Mogens go first up the street and into the yard. Then he walked slowly past the Ferry Inn, his legs like lead, his breathing rasping in his throat like sandpaper. He stood by the staircase for a while, then went to the top. In the kitchen his mother was making breakfast. He entered quietly, she was standing by the worktop humming and enjoying being on her own and he went up behind her, dripping on to the floor, and maybe that was what she heard as she suddenly turned round and was so startled that Arvid felt himself go cold too.

'Jesus! What a shock you gave me! Don't you get it, coming in like that you give people a fright.'

She stared him in the eye.

'Look at you, boy! You're soaked to the skin. Oh, Arvid, not again!'

'What do you mean?'

She ran her fingers through her hair. 'No, what *do* I mean? Nothing,' she said, and he gave her the bag.

'Look, here's dinner.'

She took the bag, peered inside, looked at him and smiled. 'I thought you were fed up with plaice?'

'It's different when you've caught them yourself,' he said, and went into the bedroom to change his clothes and maybe sleep a little, for he was more tired now than he had ever been.

AS THOUGH THEY DIDN'T EXIST

And then came the rain, for days and nights, and it never stopped. The flat they lived in shrank around Arvid and the bright houses outside turned dark and glistening and then almost invisible. He tried going outside, but the air was drenched from pavement to sky, and clouds and air merged into one and walking along the street was like wading through porridge. No one was out and no one was cycling either because the wind was strong and you got wet from your neck down into your underpants and your boots, whichever way you turned. The rain swept in like breakers up and down the streets and you couldn't say where the wind was actually coming from. The flags across the main street cracked like gunshots in a film and echoed in the emptiness between the houses, and display cases left on the pavements were hurled against the walls and made a clattering noise.

In Lodsgade everything was afloat. On his only venture outside, Arvid stood in the gateway watching the water swell up to the second step of the dairy shop. No customers dared approach, so instead they stayed at home and had juice for breakfast.

Billegaard the glazier's van came down the opposite side of the street, the muddy water swirling around its wheels. It stopped and the driver and his gofer opened the doors and walked round the van and began to untie a huge sheet of glass from the side, they fumbled with cold fingers and then they carefully lifted it down and walked unsteadily towards the gate of the glazier's workshop. They couldn't see the tarmac beneath their feet, nor the kerb. The leading man tripped just as a gust of wind came down the street and ripped the glass out of their hands. It took off and sailed through the air like a flash in the sky and Arvid could see the sky right through it, and the sky was grey, as everything else was grey. The glass landed flat on the water and stayed intact and drifted down the street like an ice floe and didn't smash until it hit the brick wall of the Ferry Inn.

The pub's cellar had turned into a pool with boxes, beer barrels and tin cans floating, and after three days of stormy weather they had to close. No one would go out for a drink in this weather anyway. In gratitude Grandmother crossed herself and said this was God's work, like THE FLOOD. Arvid watched her sitting in the chair by the window looking down on the street, nodding her head, moving her lips. Now that she had an audience all day long she sang more psalms than usual and it was unbearable, for the living room was the only place where they could gather and no one but Grandfather left the house. Every morning he put on his oilskins and wading boots and went downstairs and up round the corner to Danmarksgade. The workshop was on higher ground than the dairy shop and it was dry there and warm between the saws and the planes and the wood shavings. But he wanted to be alone.

Arvid examined the bookshelves one more time. There was nothing else to do. He started one of Leonard Strömberg's books, but after a few pages he gave up. It was easy to see that the bad guy, the wealthy landowner's son, was going to be good and a Christian at the end of the book and marry the kind-hearted, poor girl who was God-fearing and always well turned out. When Arvid was about to put the book back on the shelf a slip of paper fell to the floor. He picked it up. It was an old telegram. Apart from the 'STOP's it said: 'CATCHING BOAT HOME THIS EVENING. NEED HELP. LENE. OSLO, 16 MARCH 1949.'

Lene, that was his mother. He put the telegram back in the book and the book back in its right place.

On the fourth day of the storms his father revealed the outcome of the secret negotiations he'd been having. He cleared a space on the table, which was covered with old newspapers and Grandmother's sheet music, and on a piece of paper he began to draw. He was going to buy a cabin. Or a summer-house. Or whatever it was. They would go together and have a look at it first, but the deal was as good as done. It was clear that the purchase was an emergency solution and no one knew where the money came from, but things couldn't carry on as they were. Then they would have to stop coming and Arvid would be sent to a children's holiday camp and that's where his mother drew the line and the reason why she had words with his father in private.

Now, if only the rain would stop, they would go out to inspect the property. Søren had gone to the shipyard in Ålborg to work there and couldn't drive them and even Arvid's father didn't feel like cycling in this weather. On the sixth day the rain stopped, but the wind was still blowing so hard a neighbour had a window blown off its hinges when trying to air the house. On the seventh day his father couldn't stand it any more, he got nervous and after lunch they all set off.

The weather came in from the Kattegat with such power that bushes and poplars were bent down by the wind and it would have sent them sprawling into the ditch if they had cycled along the harbour and up the coast. So they made a detour through town, up the main street until they turned off by the railway station, along the park, where the wind rushed through the beech trees and made them creak, and on through a new neighbourhood. These were detached houses, most of them made from light brown bricks, some whitewashed with thatched roofs like the old farmhouses Arvid had seen many times. But there were no sway-backed ridges here or yellow-stained walls. Everything was straight and white and on the roofs not a single reed was out of place. One of the houses even had a swimming pool in the garden, although it was less than a ten-minute walk to the nearest beach.

'This is where the rich people live,' his father said, pointing around him. 'Every town has a neighbourhood like this.'

In Oslo it was up in the Holmenkollen hillside behind the town and Arvid had never been there until the Sunday two years ago when Sveen walked along the houses in Veitvet knocking on the doors where there were children. He mustered them on the flagstones in front of their houses and asked the parents whether it was all right if he took them to an alternative Sunday School. They couldn't go through life in ignorance, he said. When Arvid's mother was certain that Sveen was sober she said yes, and then the other parents said yes too.

Not many of the children went to Sunday School. Arvid was one of the few who had been, he had gone there almost every Sunday for a long time and got a red star on his card to prove it and a gold star for every fifth time and on the front of the card there was a colour picture of Jesus and the little children that had come unto him. But Arvid stopped when his little brother died and it was a long time ago now.

The Blåmann lorry stood ready in the road and Sveen

lifted them up one by one on to the back and finally covered them with a tarpaulin in case it should rain.

'Everyone sitting comfortably?' he said.

'YES!' they answered as one, and Sveen got behind the wheel and started the engine and it climbed up to Trondheimsveien as they knelt and peered through holes in the tarpaulin and waved to the people they knew.

They told jokes and laughed and sang songs on their way down the hill to the town. Everything they saw from the back of the lorry was familiar: the wooded ridges behind Slettaløkka and the floodlights on Bjerke trotting course, the Sinsen junction roundabout and Sinsen Cinema, where he had seen *Apache Chief*, and Ringen Cinema, where he had seen *The Mark of Zorro*. It was part of their lives all the way down to the Beer Man on the front of Schous Brewery towards the River Aker and New Bridge. But when they drove up Karl Johans Gate and past the Royal Palace they stopped singing although everyone had seen it before in pictures and once in the flesh the year Veitvet School had joined the great 17 May procession. At Majorstua they went silent. Blåmann with the tarpaulin fastened down was a prairie wagon on its way into Indian territory and Arvid and Gry and the others were the new settlers peeping cautiously out into a foreign land, where the enemy lurked behind every tree and every house. It wasn't that people looked different, they *were* different.

And Sveen drove on. Along the Holmenkollen train line and up the hill that got steeper and steeper until they arrived at the Holmenkollen ski jump, which only Jon Sand had seen close-up when he went with his father to cheer on Toralf Engan and Torgeir 'Ski-tip Licker' Brandtzæg. Sveen stopped and got out of the lorry.

'Stay where you are,' he said, tearing off the tarpaulin, for he wanted them to have a proper view. And it wasn't raining, the sky was closer here and big and very blue and there were no ski jumpers on Holmenkollen, but there was a small lake at the bottom of the ski jump. It looked all wrong.

Sveen got back into the lorry and Blåmann trundled slowly down the winding roads and this was where the houses were, big houses, posh houses. On a bend he pulled into the side of the road and parked and went behind the lorry and lifted them down one by one. They huddled together looking all around them. They looked down the sloping hillside and they saw the Oslo Fjord clearly, and Arvid even thought he could make out the Bunne Fjord, and far in the distance there was smoke coming from factory chimneys even though it was Sunday.

'So, this is where the upper class lives,' Sveen said. 'You'd better have a good look now. It will be a long time before I do a trip like this again. It's bad for me.'

They did have a good look, but they were ill at ease

and could not decide whether they should go up the hill or down and so they just stood huddled together in the same spot.

Almost all the houses had garages with cars in them, and they had big lawns too and bushes and trees and hedges that had been trimmed like poodles. In one of the gardens there was a man with a bare chest wearing shorts with a crease in. His hair was nearly white, but his body was as brown as a berry and he was holding a glass in one hand and a pair of shears in the other. He waved to them with the shears and walked towards the hedge by the road. They kept close together and didn't wave back and Sveen ignored the man.

'It's not hard,' he said, 'there's no art in being envious of these people and their money. It's dead easy. And it's not that they don't work. Some of them work like mad. But so do I. That's not the point. The point is that they own everything. The art . . .' Sveen said, and then seemed to tire. He went quiet and stood there with his mouth half open, and the tanned man came closer with a curious smile on his face.

'*I want to go home*,' Arvid whispered to Gry.

Sveen coughed and continued: 'The art', he said, 'is always to know that they are here and at the same time live your life as though they didn't exist.'

'Is that a difficult art?' Gry said. She was the only child who had said anything.

'Yes, it is,' Sveen said, and he looked like he was one of those who had tried to live that way and failed.

The man was up by the hedge now and called to them: 'Hello there, kids!'

Sveen twisted his mouth, chewed his lower lip and ran a hand through his hair. 'All right, we're off,' he said, and they shuffled towards the lorry, taking very small steps because they were moving in a close pack. Arvid could feel irritation creeping up his legs and suddenly they started kicking each other.

'In the name of Jesus!' Gry shouted. 'Let's go home, shall we!'

They sat at the back and Blåmann was on the move again, but no one felt like singing, even when they were far up Trondheimsveien on their own side of town.

Arvid looked around and could feel himself getting annoyed again when he thought about that drive, and he pedalled harder and leaned into the wind and tried to stay right behind his father without getting too close to his rear mudguard. They cycled as fast as they could alongside the pavement with its alternate light and dark kerbstones. He knew that Sveen was right and he knew there were many people in Veitvet who yearned for a house like the ones here and in Holmenkollen in Oslo, but Arvid didn't. He didn't hate them either, he just didn't want to see them. They were unimportant in an irksome way.

They left the neighbourhood and crossed the city boundary. Arvid laughed to himself as the landscape opened up and was yellow and green and gentle. There was just the road and the unploughed fields on both sides without a single tree and he thought if he cycled alone here and there was thunder and lightning, he was the highest point for a kilometre at least and it sent shivers down his spine.

They were no more than two metres above sea level and yet it looked like a mountain plateau. There could have been cloudberries growing in the heath beside the road and maybe a herd of wild reindeer coming in from the west. His whole body ached to see large animals moving at speed, see them flying along with flared nostrils, looking far into the distance, surging past with their antlers pointing to the sky.

The wind swept across the fields, pushing at their backs, almost lifting their bikes over the bumps in the pitted tarmac and all you had to do was stay on an even keel, and then the road turned east towards the coast and the wind hit them in the chest and they had to stand on the pedals to keep moving. Coming round the bend Gry's hair came loose from her slide and it whirled around and covered her face and her bike wobbled blindly towards the ditch alongside the road, but at the last moment she cleared it away and her blonde hair was caught by the wind and flew yellow against a stand of green trees.

Between the trunks they saw the sea rushing in with its white-crested tips and the lighthouse to the south. In front of the trees was a line of low buildings with corrugated iron roofs. The wind brought the smell to them long before they got there and it was strong and unpleasant. They wrinkled their noses and held their breath.

'Mink farms,' his mother laughed, and Arvid remembered the small, slim animals with marble-round eyes, how they ran up and down the wire netting of their cages in line after line and never settled, for they were going to be mink coats for wealthy women. They cycled past the buildings and Arvid didn't look back.

Beside the trees a path ran north. Arvid had been there before, with Mogens, and they were not far from the creek and the fields with the bull, they had just come a different way down and he knew there were lots of tiny summerhouses there. The trees were pines and they were smaller and more crooked than those in Norway and bent by the winds.

They passed a brown cabin, which was small but cosy, his mother said, and a green one the size of an outside loo and a yellow one which wasn't bad, but most of them looked like they had cardboard walls.

They were sheltered from the wind now, and it was easier to cycle. They turned down a narrow path with pine bushes on either side and wheel ruts that were overgrown a long time ago, no one had been down here for years.

Then there was another bend. In the middle of a small plot was a greyish-white summer-house which someone had painted fake timbers on, though the paint had almost completely peeled. It was smaller than the living room at home and the whole plot was covered in weeds and rushes up to your chest and a rainwater puddle the size of a swimming pool blocked the way to the house. They could hear frogs croaking by the puddle and Arvid saw things moving in the tangle. He squatted to see what was down there.

His father got off his bike and pushed it as far as he could. He scratched his unshaven summer face.

'Well, this is it,' he said.

'Sweet Jesus,' said Gry. She had just been confirmed. She had asked for a Tandberg tape recorder as a gift and got it, and she hadn't been to church since.

'Christ, Frank,' his mother said, 'it's just a shed!'

'My name's Frank Jansen, not John D. Rockefeller,' his father said wearily and his mother said: 'No one knows that better than me,' and they listened to the wind and the frogs croaking and then she said: 'I didn't mean that.'

It was true. She never complained about money. Why would she? It made no sense, like sneezing in the Gobi Desert and expecting someone to say 'Bless you.'

'Do we have to cut the grass?' Arvid said. 'I like it as it is.'

His mother sent him a withering look and his father

mumbled: 'We could perhaps wait and see if we could find something better.'

'Let's have no more waiting,' his mother said. 'I'm sick of waiting. I don't think I've ever done anything else. We're moving in on Wednesday!' And with that she put down her bike and waded across the puddle sending water everywhere. It wasn't deep and they were wearing boots, but the mud at the bottom was soft and slippery and they sank into it almost to the tops of their boots. When they reached the door his father took a bunch of keys from his pocket and unlocked it. He had to pull and push for the door was jammed and there was a loud creaking sound as it came free and the smell of mould hit them.

There was one small room containing four bunks with straw mattresses and an even smaller kitchen with two gas jets, and in the living room there was space for two chests of drawers and a dining table and a divan. The furniture was already there and didn't seem very solid and on the wall hung a nautical map of the Kattegat and pictures so dusty that no one could work out what they were supposed to be. Arvid went over and wiped one of them with his hand. A lighthouse.

'Yuck!' Gry cried from the kitchen. 'The cupboard and the bread bin are full of creepy-crawlies!'

Arvid sneezed and wiped the dust off his nose and left black marks on his cheek.

'Do we have to wait until Wednesday?' he said.

A SKINNY BOY IN SHORT TROUSERS

Arvid sat in the grass with his back to the summer-house wall. With one hand he was pulling up clumps of grass until he found a long blade that he placed between his thumbs. He put his thumbs to his mouth and blew. Not a sound. He licked his lips and tried again. A tiny squeak.

There were molehills everywhere and he watched his grandfather dragging a hosepipe across the lawn. Grandfather unscrewed the sprinkler and fixed one end of the hose to the exhaust pipe of his moped. The other end he stuffed down one of the holes and he went over to the moped and started it and exhaust fumes pumped out of the pipe, through the hose and into the hole. The moped chugged away in the sun and after five minutes Grandfather pulled up the hose and stuffed it into another. And so he kept on.

His father came from the bike shed carrying a pair of old shears. He was going to cut the hedge. It was just a little hedge facing a field, but no one had trimmed it in years. His father didn't like hedges, he liked spruce trees. You didn't trim spruce trees. He didn't like poodles either, he liked Alsatians and he had had one before the

War. When he saw what Grandfather was doing he walked over, said something sharp, pointing to the ground and stabbing angrily with his finger. Arvid couldn't hear what he said because of the moped, but Grandfather just turned his back on him and his father's hand stopped in mid air.

Arvid had seen a mole one time. They had cut the grass against his will and raked it into a big pile, and when they later took it away there was a mole underneath. It was still alive when they found it, but it died in the sun like the troll in the fairytale, though it was so much smaller. It looked like an animal in a cartoon. Now the moles were dying down below in their tunnels. He could hear them coughing.

He blew hard on the blade of grass, the sound pierced the sunshine and then the blade split and the sound was gone.

People died all the time, so why not animals? Old Larsen, who lived in the place they used to call the bully house back home, lay dying next to his stick, face down on the tarmac, his glasses smashed, on the slope down to the Veitvet waterfall. Arvid had been on his way to school, it was five to eight in the morning and he was running down the long set of steps by the waterfall to Rådyrveien. Larsen lay completely still on the ground and what Arvid could see of his cheek was blue beneath the grey bristles. The only thing moving was the wind through his thin hair.

It wasn't possible to walk on past him, although there was plenty of room on the footpath and the free breakfast at school started at eight on the dot. So he had to turn back and make a long detour and then he arrived too late and was told off and no one believed him when he said it was because there was a dead man lying on the road.

Little brother died. But he was born three months early in the lift up at Ullevål Hospital. He wasn't much longer than Arvid's school ruler and weighed less than a bag of sugar and they put him in a glass box called an incubator and after a week they sent his mother home, telling her to forget the whole business. But she couldn't. His father had been away, and there was no money for a bus. So every other day she walked down Trondheimsveien to town and through town up to the hospital to look through the glass of the incubator. Truls they called him, just in case, and Arvid, who had wished for a little brother, prayed to God every night to let him live, but he died anyway three months later on what could have been his birthday.

'It was as though he never existed, a dream, almost,' his mother said. But it wasn't, even though no one talked about him afterwards and his father, who was working in Sweden at the time, didn't find out until he came home.

Uncle Jesper died the year Arvid was born. Jesper was his mother's elder brother and when he died Jesper was the same age as Jesus was when he died on the cross. But Jesper was no Jesus, his mother said, for even though he was a bit of a lad, he was a lad in the same way that Tom Sawyer was, and he had lots of friends. Jesus had only twelve and a couple of them weren't much to write home about.

Everyone liked Jesper, and Arvid did too, but he had never met him.

He stood up from the grass when Gry arrived on her bike. Her hair was a yellow flag, her shorts were green and her long legs brown with light-coloured down. She was his sister Gry and yet so unfamiliar, he didn't know her.

She jumped off her bike while it was still moving, her teeth white against her tanned face when she smiled and said: 'Hi, Arvid, what are you up to?' and she turned and took the bathing towel from the luggage rack and walked towards the bike shed with the towel over her shoulder.

'Nothing,' he said, with his back to her, and straight afterwards Mogens arrived, his hair still wet and dry sand down his arms, his shirt open at the front, and he waved to Arvid as he cycled past following Gry.

Arvid went into the summer-house and looked in the mirror hanging just inside the door. When he stroked his hair from his forehead he looked like Jesper. They were both Italians, both different. Once when his mother and Gry and Arvid were down on the beach and Arvid was sitting on his own building a sandcastle, a woman went over to his mother and said: 'So kind of you to take in a refugee.'

Arvid had looked around, he didn't realise that it was him she meant, until his mother told his father the story afterwards.

'You look like Jesper,' she said, 'to a T.' Everyone on the Danish side of the family said that, and when Arvid saw pictures of Jesper as a boy, he ran his fingers over the smooth photographs of a skinny boy in short trousers with a sun-tanned face and dark hair, and if he looked long enough he could see what they meant.

'When you think about it, what happened was probably written in the stars,' his mother said after Jesper died and they had all stopped crying. She said that many times later too, but chose to leave out what had happened and Arvid didn't dare ask, even when he was old enough. Thirty-three was quite old after all, and you knew that if you looked so much like someone and everything was written in the stars, at least nothing was going to happen before then. He still had plenty of time.

Jesper had been a typesetter and a trade-union man. His grandfather had left him *Pelle the Conqueror*, and when he took his apprenticeship exams there was a picture of him in the local newspaper. The cutting was in a shoebox with his death notice and a pile of photographs. In the picture Jesper was sitting in front of the typesetting machine and he looked as if he knew what he was doing. A man was leaning over his shoulder. He was the foreman, and while Jesper was looking at his hands, as he was supposed to, the foreman was looking at the photographer and his blank face made it clear he knew nothing about anything.

But Jesper did.

That was obvious from everything his mother said about him. She had missed Jesper for as long as Arvid had been alive.

'That's many years ago now.'

He gave a start and turned away from the mirror. She was sitting by the wobbly table in the tiny living room with her chin in her hands, a book open in front of her, looking out of the window at the field, where a partridge was pecking at the ground. On the wall behind her hung a picture of a woman on a beach. The woman had a kerchief around her head and was waving to a fishing boat heading out through the breakers. The wind was blowing in the picture and two earwigs were crawling across the wall and were gone behind the picture frame.

'What was?'

'When Jesper died.'

'Twelve years ago,' Arvid said, and again they were having the same thought.

'He was so wild, but he was kind too. When I was fourteen he took me to a dance at the Ferry Inn and introduced me as his girlfriend. You can imagine how jealous the other girls were. He was so popular. He gave me a beer too. That didn't taste so good, but it was a wonderful evening.'

She laughed. 'I had to be smuggled into my bedroom afterwards. It was past twelve o'clock.'

Jesper was a resistance man during the War, one of the first in town.

'It took time before it kicked off in Denmark, longer than in Norway, but when it did, it really happened and Jesper was glad. He was as wild during the War as he had been before, he took risks all the time and when things went wrong he had to escape in a fishing boat to the coast of Sweden. Your grandfather was furious as always, but the crew told us later that Jesper sat by himself, laughing all the way,' and all this made the boats in the harbour look different when Arvid walked with his bike along the piers, inspecting them and wondering what they looked like inside and where Jesper had been hiding.

In 1945 Jesper was one of the men who walked down Danmarksgade with a machine gun slung over his shoulder and he had looked around at all the people on the pavement and smiled at them and he was happy because the War was over and because he was still alive, and that made the streets seem new and brighter as Arvid pedalled through them, and not as sleepy and full of rubbish.

He walked over to the little bookcase and took out the book about Klit Per, which his mother had borrowed from the library, and lay down on the divan to read.

'For someone who likes reading so much you should

do something with *words* when you grow up,' his mother said.

Typesetter, Arvid thought, and Gry came in through the open door and said: 'Is it all right if I go to the cinema with Mogens?'

'Yes, it is,' his mother said, looking at Arvid, but he pretended not to hear and turned a page in the book. Gry went out to Mogens, who was waiting by the door.

'Arvid?' his mother said.

'Yes?'

'No, no, nothing.'

'Well, what the hell,' Arvid said.

He lay reading. Klit Per was a young fishing hand on the west coast. He had big poles that he used when he fought against anyone who tried to harass him after his parents died and he alone had to take care of the little ones in the family and put bread on the table.

There was a clink of metal on stone outside the door and his father came in from the sun shading his eyes and his face was dark.

'What's up with you?' his mother said.

'The damn hedge,' he said, but Arvid knew that wasn't true. It was the moles. His father was a softie.

THERE WAS A REEK OF DEAD BODIES

The circular saw could cut a man in two. Arvid had thought about it many times and it wasn't funny, but he thought about it anyway. If you placed a man on the board and he opened his legs you could slice him from crotch to forehead, and then Arvid had to stop, for in truth, you couldn't really think about it.

But that was during the day. At night the saw whined through his dreams, the man howled, there was a reek of dead bodies and ground bone and Arvid screamed so loud the little room swelled with the sound.

The straw mattresses and old newspapers creaked as the others turned in their bunks. Between the mattresses and the wire netting there were old newspapers they hadn't changed yet, and there they could read that the whole world was sighing with relief because Stalin had died in Moscow.

'Was that you, Arvid?' His father's voice sounded distant and strangely weary.

'Yes.' His head hurt, his lips were dry and it was difficult to talk.

'What is it?'

'There's a reek of dead bodies,' he said into the darkness, and he felt sick too.

He heard his father's hand rummaging over the bedside table to find the matches they used for the paraffin lamp. It took him a long time, but in the end he found them and there was a dry scraping noise as he opened the box.

His mother turned in her bunk and coughed loudly as if she was going to be sick.

'Wait a minute,' she said. 'That's not dead bodies. That's gas.'

His father sprang out of bed and when his feet hit the floor he fell to his knees. 'What the hell,' he mumbled and started to crawl towards the kitchen. It was slow work and they could hear him throwing up on the kitchen floor. They should have got out of bed, but they lay there waiting, without the will to move.

'The gas is on,' his father said to himself, and his mother pulled herself together and struggled to her feet and she leaned over the top bunk and shook the duvet.

'Gry! Wake up!' Gry didn't stir and his mother shook her again.

'I want to sleep,' Gry mumbled, and his mother pulled at the duvet and it slipped off her body and on to the floor.

'Come on now,' his mother said, 'or else we'll die.'

Carefully she gave Gry a hand down, and then she helped Arvid. He felt heavy and lumpen.

'I'm going to be sick,' he whispered.

'Be sick then, but keep moving,' his mother said, and he grabbed her nightdress and threw up all over his pyjamas and the rag rug on the way into the living room. His father was on his feet, shaking the door. It was stuck in the frame and he was too weak to push it open.

'Goddamn it,' he groaned, took a run-up and hit it with what force he had left. The door flew open with a ripping sound and they tumbled out on to the grass. The air was like fresh water on their faces.

They lay in the grass beside each other breathing heavily, looking up at the deep blue night sky. It was starry and the air was cool. Arvid saw the Plough and the Great Bear, but then there was a throbbing behind his eyes and he rose out of himself, higher and higher, until he was flying round their plot like a helicopter, round and round in big circles. He could see the whole family far below, there were four patches of light bedwear against the darker grass in the middle of a great carousel. He saw the fields and the pine trees and the Skagen railway line to the north like a bright jet of light, and the sea, vast and calm close by. He thought maybe he should wave to them, but then he sank back down, the dew drenched his pyjamas and his teeth began to chatter.

'Good thing we've got a draughty old cabin,' Gry said, 'or we would be dead now.'

'Who'd have thought we would be thankful for that,' his father said. His chest rose and fell, rose and fell. 'What time is it?'

'Three.'

'Well, I should have been up by now anyway. I've got such a lot to do,' he said, and laughed out loud until he had to throw up and Arvid's mother only laughed a little, she coughed and said: 'What's happening to this family?'

'Nothing,' his father said. 'Nothing's happening to this family.' Arvid heard a sharp crunch as his father crushed the box of matches he still held in his hand.

'Maybe not,' his mother said, and coughed again. She staggered to her feet and stood there until she had stopped being sick and then she went into the cabin and opened the windows all the way round and came back out with warm clothes for all four of them. Her face was red after holding her breath for so long.

'We won't be able to go in there for a while,' she said. 'You'll have to walk around a bit to keep yourselves warm.' They were freezing cold now and quickly dressed on the grass and Gry tugged at Arvid's arm.

'Come on, let's go to the beach. It will be nice there now.'

They walked down between the rows of pine trees and across a beach plot, where the house was dark and empty, and along a path to the shore. It was easy to find their way for the moon was shining, clear and yellow, even though they couldn't see it from where they were, but all the way down they could hear the sea.

They still felt a little shaken and Gry said: 'Just imagine if we'd died.'

'We wouldn't have. Not me anyway.'

'How do you know?'

'I just know.'

Gry looked at him and shook her head. 'You're pretty weird sometimes, you know that?' she said.

They scrambled over some pine-tree roots and then they stopped. Before them lay the sea, dark, and you could hear the soft hiss of it and right above them hung the moon, a huge, yellow balloon. How big it is, Arvid thought. The beams from the lighthouse seemed weak and almost meaningless by comparison.

'Isn't it pretty?' Gry said, sitting on a low sand dune. She caught her hair with both hands, formed it into a ponytail and laid it over one shoulder. He saw her white neck and her hair reached down to her stomach, and her hair glowed and her neck glowed and Arvid thought, now I see what Mogens sees. He felt as light as air. He wanted to touch her, but he couldn't and then he did anyway. Her skin was warm and her neck curved and fitted well into his hand, but his hand was cold, and she shivered and hunched up her shoulders right away and he withdrew his hand.

'Hey, what are you doing?'

'I don't know,' he said, and must have looked startled for she smiled and nudged him and said: 'Take it easy.

Your hand was just cold. It was OK. Honestly.' But that didn't help, he couldn't say anything and felt shaky again and slipped away from her, down the dune and walked towards the water.

'Where are you going?' she said, but he didn't answer.

He walked right down to the sea, there was a high tide and the belt of sand was slimmer than usual, and the moon was on the water and nothing cast a shadow except himself until he came to the rushes. They were like a wall and so high he couldn't see over them, but the path continued straight on. He followed it and knew exactly where he was. Now he could hear the gulls, it was like a humming, but he couldn't see them. There was a murmur in the rushes but that was the creek and he walked on until the rushes were not so tall any more and faded away and he saw the fields sloping down in front of him and then the moon vanished behind a large cloud and he stopped.

It was pitch black. He stood still on the path and waited for his eyes to adapt. He heard someone or something trampling and snorting. It was hard to know where the sound was coming from, it kept moving and a beam of light from the lighthouse swept in across the land and that was when he saw it, a large, black body in front of him. He took two steps back and the beam swept by and the night became even darker and swirled around him full of sounds and he turned and ran. He was naked with only his skin between him and all that could come out of nowhere and harm him, tear him to pieces while still alive.

In the darkness he must have lost his way because he ran straight into the sea with a splash: it wasn't deep, but it was shockingly cold and full of mud and he tried counting to ten and then breathing slowly to stop the wild shivers that were rising up his spine. He bent down and groped with his hands and found his way back, calmer now until he bumped into something soft and living and he groaned aloud. The moon shone out again. It was Gry.

'Hey, Arvid, you look as if you have been in the wars. How did you get so mucky?'

'I saw something out there.'

'Just a cow. I saw it too.'

'I thought it was the bull,' he said. His throat burned and he wiped his face and got mud on his jumper.

'But you're not afraid of the bull, are you? Mogens told me about you and the bull. That was some story.'

Mogens had told her about the bull. Mogens told her everything.

'That was during the day. It was light then.' He began to shake and his teeth were chattering.

'My lovely brother,' Gry said, and hugged him, muck and all. She stroked his back and he wanted to run away, but he couldn't move. She was softer and taller than he was. He hugged her and held her neck in his hand and wondered if he should cry or not.

'I didn't think you were afraid of anything,' she said. 'My lovely weird little brother.'

She held her arm around him as they walked towards the dune and up the path across the beach plot, but when they came to the row of pine trees he gently removed her arm.

The sky changed colour from deep blue to a lighter blue, the moon paled and the stars were barely visible. When they reached their summer-house his father was nowhere to be seen and his mother was standing just inside the door with a broom in her hand sweeping thin air impatiently towards the open door. The broom didn't touch the floor and there was nothing there to see.

'She's away with the fairies,' Gry said, 'but then what can you expect?'

His mother turned and said angrily: 'Very funny. Propane gas is heavier than air, right? You take the broom!' She gave it to Arvid and he swept and swept without seeing a thing and so he didn't know if he had finished or not and he felt like an idiot.

'Can we come back in now?' he said.

'That should be fine.'

'OK.' He placed the broom against the door and went in and sniffed the kitchen. The rubber pipe to the gas had been detached and the empty container was by the wall. They could say what they liked. There was a reek of dead bodies.

HARD AS FLINT

Aunt Else lived to the south of town. It was a long bike ride there, from the summer-house along the coast and through the town centre, for the annual visit. From her living-room window Arvid could see the Kattegat, with the bay facing Sæby and one mole sticking out into the sea and disappearing to the north like a line drawn in charcoal. Aunt Else was Grandmother's elder sister. She was taller than Grandmother, who was very small and sparrow-like, and Aunt Else's hair was still black with grey streaks. Arvid liked her. Although she went to church every Sunday she was still easy to talk to.

All the houses in her street were small and painted yellow with red-tiled roofs and in Aunt Else's living room the walls were covered with pictures and old photographs and nautical charts and objects from fishing boats. Aunt Else was a fisherman's wife, everyone who lived here was connected with fishing and always had been. Twenty years ago the fishing smack *Lise-Lotte* sank north of Skagen with Aunt Else's husband on board. It was wartime then and a dark, moonless night and stormy weather, even the sky had its blackout blinds up, and nothing from the wreck was ever found.

It was Aunt Else who hid Jesper until he could escape to Sweden. They were good friends even though she was his aunt and since then she had lived alone. The only thing she regretted was that she and her husband had waited too long to have children, and then Jesper had died, and anyway it had been too late for a long time, for she was sixty-five now. For a while she thought of doing what Madame Olsen did in *Pelle the Conqueror*, but she was afraid her husband would turn up one fine day like Boatman Olsen did in the book and so she didn't take the risk.

'Mark my words, young man, it was not for the lack of candidates!' She laughed and Arvid laughed because it was easy to see that Aunt Else had been attractive in a way that was not usual in this town. Her eyes were big and brown and her black hair with the grey streaks and her narrow face made you think of other countries than Denmark.

In front of the house was a small lawn, with the beach directly below, and there were white chairs and a table where they could sit and eat cake, when the wind was not too strong. Grandmother and Grandfather had already arrived and Grandmother was sitting in one of the chairs with a blanket wrapped around her hips and thighs. Small and fragile like a baby bird, she seemed ten years older than Aunt Else, her eyes were blue and transparent and she looked at Arvid with a smile on her lips and he couldn't work out why she was smiling.

Arvid ate cake. When he had finished the first piece Aunt Else said: 'Surely you're not going to have just one piece, are you?' He surely wasn't, and he took another slice of layer cake and Grandmother frowned at him as if it was bad manners to eat more than one piece. What the hell, he thought, and left the table and walked down to the water with the piece of cake in his hand. Grandfather had been standing there all the time, hands behind his back, wearing the not-so-worn suit and a tie, and the stub of a cigar poked out from under his moustache.

'Don't you want some cake, Granddad?' Arvid said, but Grandfather shook his head without turning and gazed across the sea. He took out the cigar and spat in the sand and put it back in and said: 'We didn't even have shoes then. Only in the winter. In the autumn, when I was in the fields with the cows, my feet were so frozen that when they had a shit I would run over and put my feet in it. That warmed them up, for a while.'

Grandfather stood smoking, and then he spat again and threw the cigar butt into the sea and walked up to the house without looking at Arvid even once. His shoulders were crooked at the top, almost like a hunchback's.

'The old miser,' Arvid mumbled.

Gry came down and joined him. She had icing sugar round her mouth, and she licked it and looked pleased.

'What's up with Granddad? He walked straight in without a word.'

Arvid shrugged and ate a mouthful of cake.

'*Pelle the Conqueror*, Part One,' he said.

'What?'

'When Granddad was a boy, he had to walk barefoot when he tended the cows, even in the autumn, and he warmed his feet in the cowpats. It's in the book too. I wonder if he really did it or he just read about it.'

'Of course he did, otherwise he wouldn't have said so.'

'Maybe he did,' Arvid said. 'I don't give a damn.'

When they went back up Grandfather was still in the house and Aunt Else had gone in after him. After a while they came out and Grandfather sat down at the table to eat cake. But he said nothing.

Aunt Else was in the doorway and called Arvid to her. He went over and she said: 'Come with me. I've got something to show you.' He followed her through the living room to the small room behind the kitchen. He had never been there before. The walls, the shelves and the windowsill were full of souvenirs of bygone days. Aunt Else opened a chest in the corner. It was brown and made of wood with a curved lid and had no decoration of any kind, just a wrought-iron handle on each side and below the keyhole you could see the numbers 1869 when the light was straight on them.

'I didn't give you anything for your birthday,' she said, and took out something big and square wrapped in a neckerchief. 'I always meant to give it to Jesper, but never got around to it and then it was too late. When the accident happened I was so sorry I hadn't.'

'What happened?' Arvid said.

'He was out sailing with a friend. There was a strong wind and Jesper was sitting at the helm. When they had to change course to go round the lighthouse island the current was so strong he lost control of the tiller and the sail flew back and the boom hit him on the head. He died instantly. Didn't you know?'

'Mother said it was written in the stars.'

Aunt Else gave a faint smile. 'Did she say that? You know, Arvid, your mother was very fond of Jesper. They were almost always together after she was old enough for him not to be embarrassed. You might say they protected each other. That's what it looked like anyway. She helped him whenever he got into trouble with your short-tempered grandfather and he helped her that time when she came home from Norway so suddenly. No one else dared. The year he died and you were born she was tired and poorly, she was back in Norway then of course. It was important for her to know that Jesper was out there somewhere. When he died her life seemed so meaning-less she had to console herself with the thought that it had not been the usual sort of accident, that it had been preordained and no one could have done anything. That's the way people think sometimes.'

'So it wasn't written in the stars then?' His hands were

clammy and he kept wiping them up and down the thighs of his trousers. The denim felt stiff to his palms.

'Nothing is written in the stars, Arvid, except that we will die, not how and certainly not *when*, and what comes afterwards we can only guess.'

She unwrapped the cloth and took out a large, white book. The cover looked like marble and there were letters on it that looked like gold.

'It's written in English. "An Artist in Italy". Meaning "En kunstner i Italia", if you translate it, but I'm sure you've learned some English at school. I was given it by my grandfather and he got it from the man who'd done the pictures in it. It was to thank him for the loan of a boat while he was on holiday here on the coast. He'd heard that my grandfather was from Italy.'

Arvid took the book. It was heavy and smooth and when he opened it on the first page he saw:

> *Open my heart, and you will see*
> *Graved inside of it, 'Italy'*

The poem was printed in a kind of handwritten style he could easily read and he knew what it said and he ran his fingertips over the letters and thought he would copy them one day.

He leafed through the book. There was a lot of difficult-looking text, but mostly it consisted of pictures, colour pictures of sun-drenched countryside and baked houses and churches and people in shabby clothes, and oranges and tall, slim trees. Cypresses they were called. One of the pictures showed the blue Bay of Naples and the town with its gleaming houses and Vesuvius high in the distance, almost floating. He held the book open at that page and studied the picture carefully and Aunt Else leaned over his shoulder.

'Yes, that's the town my grandfather came from. Naples. His name was Bruno.'

'I know.' He closed the book and got up. 'Thank you very much,' he said.

He stood for a moment and then he shook Aunt Else's hand and bowed, but she bent forward and gave him a hug. She smelled like her house smelled. He put the book under his arm and they went back to the living room. It was a nice room when the sun shone in through the windows, the crossbars in the frame making square patterns on the floor, and the others were sitting outside at the garden table, they were bathed in light, his father's shirt was a dazzling white, Gry's hair gleamed and Grandmother stood behind his mother ready to pour coffee in her cup, but his mother pushed the pot away so hard that Grandmother spilled coffee on the tablecloth. The stain glinted in the sun.

Aunt Else placed both hands on Arvid's shoulders and gazed out of the window.

'She's been trying so hard to make amends. It just isn't that easy. She looks gentle and fragile, but she's hard as flint.'

'Who is?'

'Kirsten. Your grandmother,' Aunt Else said, and Arvid remembered the time there was a knock at the door in Lodsgade and he and Grandmother were alone over the milk shop and two men were outside wanting to have a word with her. They came up the stairs and stood on the landing by the kitchen and began to talk about God and the Day of Judgement. They were Jehovah's Witnesses. Grandmother listened to them without uttering a word. Finally there was a silence and they didn't know what more to say, for the tiny woman with the pale blue eyes was looking right through them and they shifted their feet and Grandmother began to talk in a low, clear voice. She talked about God and Jesus and the Holy Spirit and she talked about the love for mankind of the one who died on the cross for our sins, and His House, which was the only House and it had many rooms, but not *that* many. She talked about the false prophets and the doubts that Thomas had, and Peter, who denied the Lord thrice before the cock crowed, and her voice was cold as ice. She talked about the angel's flaming sword and about Abraham, who would sacrifice Isaac for his belief in God, and Job, who didn't understand what really counted until he had lost everything and there was frost in the air in the stairwell.

The two men backed down the steps and stopped halfway and tried to get a word in, but Grandmother wasn't listening any more and her words were like blows from a cane, for they had a different view from her about what was right and what was wrong and she was hard as flint and turned people from her door if they had stumbled from the path.

When Aunt Else and Arvid came out, his mother was sitting with her face buried in her arms on the table, crying. His father was beside her with his hand raised stiffly in the air above her neck and then he shook his head as though he had just woken up and lowered his arm gently around her shoulders. She straightened up at once and shouted: 'Don't you touch me! I don't need you on my side now. I needed you *then*! Now it's too late!' And his father turned to stone in his chair.

Arvid looked at Gry, but she was sitting with her back to him, staring across the bay, her hair hanging down quite still, like a yellow wall. He turned to his grandfather.

'Grandfather, have you read *Pelle the Conqueror*?' he said in a loud voice and his words hung in the air like a black cloud. Grandfather touched his moustache, stroked it with his index finger and looked around. No one said anything and his mother stopped crying.

'Have you?' he said, even louder.

'It's in the bookcase. Of course I have,' Grandfather said.

'You never warmed your feet in the cowpats, did you? You just read about it!'

'What nonsense, Arvid,' Grandfather said. 'I've just told you—'

'You're lying!' screamed Arvid. 'You're just a senile old man!'

'Come now, Arvid,' his mother said, and started to walk across the lawn and Arvid backed away a few steps and shouted: 'He's so damn senile!' and turned away to run with the book under his arm, but by then his mother had reached him and she held him back.

A STORM ROUND CAPE HORN

He woke up early, before the others, climbed down from his bunk with the mattress not creaking and went into the living room. The brick floor was cold to the touch and he curled up his toes as he got dressed. They kept their swimming clothes in the dresser by the door. He took out his red trunks and a big towel and then he went over to his mother's bag on the divan, put in a hand and pulled out a Cooly from the pack and a matchbox with Tordenskjold's face on it without shaking it once. He placed the cigarette, the matchbox and the trunks on the towel and rolled it up tight and put it under his arm. In the kitchen he took a biscuit from the table and placed it between his teeth.

The door was more difficult, but if he held the handle and at the same time pushed hard he could open it without a squeak.

The sun was up, the sky still a pale blue, the grass was dewy and left damp marks on his yellow gym shoes. He ate the biscuit as he walked down between the pine trees, over the gravel path and the beach plot. The empty summer-house didn't look empty now, there were flowery curtains in the window and the sun lit them up, it was Sunday and tomorrow his father was going home.

When he got to the beach he took off his gym shoes. The sand was cool and fine-grained against the soles of his feet. He held the shoes in his hands and walked through the water to the first sandbank, which was broad now and high above the sea. It was low tide and he walked along the sandbank until he came to the creek and waded across. It was deeper here, his shorts got wet at the bottom, the brackish water was cold and the slimy riverbed oozed between his toes, whirled up and made the water murky.

He walked on down the beach along by the rushes until he came to a sheltered clearing. The wind wasn't blowing and the sea was dead calm, there was no one around, but he didn't want to change clothes on the open beach. Out by the lighthouse there was a morning mist above the calm sea and the whole island hovered in the air like a Zeppelin.

He unrolled his towel and laid it across the sand and sat down and took off his jumper and shorts. He folded the shorts with the wet patch up so it could dry in the sun. He pulled off his underpants and quickly wriggled into his trunks and stood up and went to the water's edge. He took a deep breath before walking into the shallows. The water was warm at first and then got colder and colder as he waded out, but he kept the same pace and didn't stop. When it was up to his stomach he launched himself.

He swam calmly, pushing powerfully with his legs and he thought about every stroke he made. He passed the second sandbank. It was so shallow the bottom scraped against his knees, but he didn't stand up because then he would start to freeze.

Beyond the third sandbank he stopped, and trod water and the water was perfectly still, everything was perfectly still, and he heard himself breathing. The water was green and deep, the sun flashed on the smooth surface and into his face and it was hard to see. He turned to land, a brown and green strip in the distance. He held his breath. There wasn't a sound anywhere. He felt an urge to sing. '*Non ho l'età / Non ho l'età per amarti / Non ho l'età per uscire,*' he sang, but it sounded so odd with his voice all on its own that he stopped and saved his breath for the trip back. He swam around a little, but couldn't see a ripple. He lay on his back and whistled and rested for a while and then he made for the shore. He kept the rhythm and breathed loudly with each stroke and stopped when his hands touched the sand.

His legs were heavy when he came ashore, but still he ran to keep himself warm. Back in the rushes he shook his towel and rubbed himself hard, stretched it out again and lay down. He was longer than the towel, his legs came over the end and he dug his heels into the sand until his feet were almost completely covered. He sat up and shovelled sand over his legs until they were no longer visible and carefully lay back. With his arms outstretched he pulled dry, white sand on to his stomach and chest and after a while the sand became darker and damp. He wriggled and squirmed so his body sank even further and he kept adding more sand and in the end only his head and his arms could be seen. He carried on until he could feel the weight of what was covering him. He thought, now I'm part of the beach.

At first the sand was cold, but the sun warmed it from the outside and his skin from the inside and he sensed it only as a firmness around his body.

He lay staring up at the sky. There was just one small cloud there. He looked at it and it dissolved and was gone. He stretched out a hand for his trousers and grasped his mother's matchbox and cigarette, slowly, so the sand wouldn't run off his shoulders and show his skin. He poked the cigarette in his mouth and with both hands he struck and held the match and lit the Cooly. He inhaled and forced himself not to cough. It didn't taste good, the menthol was out of place here on the beach and the smoke smarted on his tongue, but he inhaled deeper with every drag. He closed his eyes and smoked and felt the sand on his skin and suddenly his body felt heavier and it spiralled down into the earth and then he had to open his eyes again.

Someone was coming. He heard sandals flip-flapping behind him somewhere and he saw her appear by the opening to the clearing where he was lying, blue dress against blue sky, he lay so still and she spotted him at once. She put her bathing things on the sand, looked out to sea and loosened a blue slide from her long, dark hair and then she turned and looked him straight in the eye.

'Oh, sorry, is this taken?'

He didn't answer and she bent down to pick up her towel and then she looked at him again and smiled.

'It's you, isn't it. I didn't recognise you without a body. You aren't out running today then?'

'No.'

'No, I suppose it must be tiring after a while.' She laughed.

He took a drag of the cigarette, forgot to concentrate and coughed. She cast her eyes over his sandy body, and he said: 'Where's your boyfriend then?'

'Boyfriend? Oh, him. Well, he was a waste of space, so he had to go. You're Norwegian, aren't you?'

'No, I'm Italian.'

'But you speak Norwegian. I can hear you do.'

'That's where I live now.'

'Oh,' she said. 'Well, you do look a bit Italian. Have you been in for a swim?'

He nodded and sand slid down his nose. He screwed up his eyes and blew it away.

'I always have a morning swim when the weather's nice,' she said. 'I'm staying in a summer-house further up, but this is the best place. It's not crowded here. Aren't you a little too young for that?' She pointed to the cigarette.

'I'm twelve,' he said, trying to make it sound like eighteen. His back itched and he wanted to turn, but the sand covering him was set, and if he did turn, it would crack and his body would be revealed. The cigarette was burning between his fingers, down to his fingertips, and suddenly it hurt and he quickly flicked it into the rushes. He felt strange, he squinted and looked at her, the blue dress waving against the sun, but there was no wind, everything around them was still and the sun burned his stomach through the sand. It felt like a red-hot patch.

'That's better,' she said. 'You're a good-looking boy. That much I can see. But twelve is a bit too young.' She laughed loudly, teasingly and walked over to him and crouched down and stroked his hair. He twisted his head and swallowed, his face was burning and the sand was like concrete on his legs and chest. He turned back and looked at her neck, it was brown and there were tiny beads of sweat in the faint, fine wrinkles that ran down to her shoulders. She kissed him on the cheek and she smelled of roses, he gasped and she stood up and said: 'I think I'll have that swim now, and let her blue dress fall to her feet. She had nothing on but a bikini bottom and she was just as brown everywhere and looked like nothing he had ever seen before. He didn't know if he could breathe any longer. She stood like a pillar before him in an instant that stretched between them and grew until she turned and went down to the water. Her spine was an unbroken line and she reached the sea and waded out, sinking as she walked and then fell forward and started swimming. He saw her dark hair against the shiny water. She didn't turn and he had to force his body up through the armour of sand. It had forgotten everything it had ever known.

When he came up to the summer-house the others were sitting at the table. His mother's eyes were swollen and red, but otherwise everything seemed calm. He went out, shook the towel and hung it over the clothes line along with his trunks. Then he went in and on his way to the table slipped the matches into the bag, which was still on the divan, and he sat down and took a slice of rye bread.

'You should have woken me,' his father said. 'Then we could have gone swimming together.' He smiled at Arvid, but Arvid just shrugged and buttered the bread and ate.

'You didn't swim too far out, did you?' his mother said. Arvid looked straight at her.

'No, I did not,' he said loudly. And then she knew he had.

Gry was as she always was, sitting with her chin in her hands, a faraway look and a yawn every three minutes. She rubbed her eyes and stretched her arms above her head. 'Hope the weather holds so we can have a nice trip,' she said.

They were going to the lighthouse. Twice a week the post boat chugged out and moored for two hours. His mother had spoken to the skipper and he said it was fine, lots of people went out with him for a small fee. His mother hadn't been there for fifteen years and she was the only person in the family who had.

Grandmother and Grandfather were going, and Mogens. The three who lived in town had decided to board in the harbour where the boat lay alongside the Læsø ferry. Arvid and the others didn't have to go that far, because when the tide was high, at twelve, the boat came to the jetty where they used to dive. Everyone was pretty keen to get out and see the coast from the sea for once and not, as always, the other way.

'Don't worry. The weather will hold,' his father said. As usual he had listened to the weather forecast. They had a portable Kurér radio on the window-sill in the living room and it was on every morning. Now it was the morning service and Arvid went over and switched it off.

'I can't eat with that racket on,' he said.

After breakfast his father went into the bunk room. There wasn't a door, only a curtain, and they could hear him rummaging around. He was packing, and was trying to do it in a discreet way, but they knew what he was up to.

At half-past eleven they fetched their bikes from the shed. His father strapped the bag with the picnic to the luggage rack and they cycled off, down the gravel road and then along by the sea. There was an offshore wind, the air was thick with the scents of the fields and the warm earth and they could see the island all the way. It was no longer floating but lay where it was supposed to.

At the jetty the boat still hadn't come, and there was no one there waiting. They placed their bikes on the stand by the green beach hut. It looked run-down when you got up close. Arvid had never seen anyone use it.

They walked slowly on to the jetty and along to the very end of it. Arvid sat down on the edge and dangled his legs, his father stood with his hands in his pockets and Gry lay on her stomach and looked down into the water. His mother picked up the pack of Cooly cigarettes, counted them twice and shook her head. She lit one and stood smoking with her eyes closed and her face to the sun. She had tanned a deep brown in a matter of weeks, her face was calm now and all of a sudden Arvid could see she was good-looking. Perhaps she always had been.

No one said anything. The sun was baking hot. Then the boat came round the headland by Tordenskjold's Redoubt. It was yellow and rode high in the water with no other cargo than the post. It was an old fishing smack that had been renovated and repainted and Arvid didn't like the colour. Jaundice yellow, he thought, and he knew it was something he had read in a book. Grandfather and Grandmother and Mogens and a woman with a rucksack stood in the bows. The skipper cut the engine and started up again in reverse to brake and the boat glided in to the jetty. The water churned at the rear, and the boat stopped perfectly, and the side of it barely touched the poles. They climbed on board and Mogens smiled at Gry.

'Hi, Goldilocks,' he said. He was wearing a blue shirt with green palm trees on, his hair was washed and combed like Tommy Steele used to have it and Gry smiled back. The boat started up again right away and Arvid went to the bows and looked down at the frothing water as the boat veered out and headed for the island. The long chimney banged and clanked and the exhaust was spat out in tiny, angry wisps. Like smoke signals, Arvid thought. There was the smell of diesel and seawater.

The trip took longer than expected. The island slowly grew in size, there were bushes and trees they hadn't known about and he had never thought there was anyone actually living on the island except for the lighthouse keeper, but as they approached he saw the roofs of houses and a little harbour. There was a yacht moored with a Swedish flag astern and they slipped in behind it and he could see small rose gardens. The houses were yellow and the roses pink and everything else was green apart from the lighthouse, which had been built with grey stone and was not as tall as it seemed from the distance. The large door was open and they could see the spiral staircase inside as they passed, it wound up to the top and disappeared into the darkness.

124

Gry and Mogens got off first and were talking as they walked up the path between the garden fences while Arvid brought up the rear. One of the houses had a bell on the roof and when he went over to the window and peered in, he saw Jesus on the cross and a ship hanging from the ceiling. In the gloom, with only the light coming from the windows, it looked life-like. The Flying Dutchman could have sailed that ship. He let the others go on ahead of him and tried the door. It was open, there wasn't even a lock and he went in and stood between the few rows of pews. He looked around and it was quiet and empty and he climbed up on one of the pews. The ship hung at an angle above him and had been beautifully made down to the tiniest detail in the rigging and on the deck, and it swayed in the draught from the open door where the sun shone a few metres in on the floor. Then the sun disappeared and there was someone standing there.

'I don't think we're allowed to come in here, Arvid,' his father said in a hushed voice and Arvid turned and saw his silhouette, a face without features, framed by the doorway. He got down from the pew, still eyeing the ship, and walked backwards and out, and his father quietly closed the door behind him.

They walked together under the trees and followed the others to a clearing. His father put his arm round Arvid's shoulders and said: 'Well, Arvid, tomorrow I'm leaving,' but Arvid didn't notice and Arvid didn't hear, for he was on the ship in a storm round Cape Horn one moonless night, the rain lashing down, everyone running about on the deck amidst torn rigging and careering barrels, the splintered wood of smashed lifeboats flying through the air, the hull groaning and the captain on the bridge yelling. The sails had to be reefed and Arvid climbed up the mainmast like a monkey, and his father removed his arm.

Grandmother had brought along a blanket and a Thermos flask of coffee and bottles of orangeade from the shop. Arvid had a bottle which he opened with his belt buckle. The orange was warm and fizzed up his nose as he drank. Everyone sat down on the blanket except for Arvid, and Grandmother's bun bobbed up and down in the sun as she handed out the goodies. He stood for a while listening to Mogens telling jokes. He was good at telling stories and all the jokes were a little close to the bone and even Grandmother chuckled. But Arvid had heard them before, he took his bottle and walked down to the water and sat behind a rock. Jesper had died on the way round this headland.

The wind was blowing enough to fill a sail, he drank the last of the pop, took a slip of paper from his trouser pocket and put it in the bottle. There was nothing written on the paper, but then no one was going to read it anyway, and he threw the bottle into the sea. It moved up and down with the waves until a gust of wind caught it and whirled it round and water got into the neck and the bottle sank. He had forgotten to put on the top.

His grandfather joined him, Arvid could hear him panting and in his mouth he had a fresh cigar. He took a couple of long drags before removing the cigar and blew smoke down his chest, coughed, scratched the back of his neck and said: 'Well, Arvid. I've read the first part of *Pelle* again three times and I still can't find it. It's not there. It simply isn't.'

That couldn't be right. He had been so sure. If he closed his eyes he could see the book in front of him and even the place on the page where he thought it was, on the left-hand side, at the bottom. He had been so sure.

Grandfather didn't look at Arvid as he spoke, but slightly to the right, past his ear. 'That's what I had to say,' he said, and turned and walked back up the path to join the others. The path was rugged and full of stones and he placed one foot carefully in front of the other. Grandfather was an old man.

The others weren't sitting any more, they had stood up from the blanket and were now bending over a heap of stones studying rare flowers. Arvid had seen them himself on his way down, but you couldn't pick them because all flowers on this island were protected, the skipper had told them that before they got off the boat.

He looked back at the coast. It was a long way off, and the town was a rust-red stripe of south-facing roofs, with the church spire and the water tower that looked like Uncle Scrooge's money bin in the early Donald Duck comics. At least that's what he had always imagined and had said so, and everyone thought that was a funny thing to say. He wondered whether it was possible to swim all the way to land. It probably was, but not for him, he would have had to train and train for many years and when those years had passed the point of it would have gone with them.

'You keep away from the boy!' he heard his mother say from above and Grandfather lifted his empty palms, still holding the cigar, and looked up at the sky.

Gry and Mogens had changed into their swimming gear and came running, but they didn't stop by him, they just kept running and jumped into the water, went under and came up again and Mogens no longer looked like Tommy Steele.

'Come on in, Arvid,' he shouted. 'It's great!'

Arvid shook his head. 'Watch out for the riptides,' he said.

'Don't talk rubbish. There are no riptides here,' Gry said, smacking her hand down hard on the water, sending the spray all the way up to the shore. Arvid shrugged and walked along the water's edge round to the headland until he came to a bay on the far side of the island. He couldn't see the coast from here, only the sea stretching out towards Sweden and a sailing boat far in the distance. The sun was baking down and he lay in the shade of a bush, closed his eyes and fell asleep at once.

When he awoke he was no longer in the shade, the skin on his face felt like cardboard and he heard someone shouting. He sat up and looked around, he was on the island, but in his dream he had been in Italy and the sun had been a burning globe.

'Is that you there?' Mogens called. He came walking along the beach, in his palm-tree shirt and his hair was dry. 'We've been looking all over for you. We have to go now. The others are waiting on the jetty.'

'I fell asleep.'

'Jesus. Is there anything wrong?'

'No, no, I just fell asleep.'

'Everything's OK? Are you sure?'

'Yes, for Christ's sake. Didn't you hear what I just said?'

'Sure I did. Anyway, we'll have to run now. The boat should've left ages ago.'

They sprinted across the island, over rocks and lyme grass and in between the trees and past the houses, past the chapel with the ship and past the lighthouse that he wouldn't be going up now and down to the little harbour. The whole family was waiting on the wooden jetty, the post boat had started the engine and his father looked furious. The Swedish yacht was gone.

When everyone was on board and the boat chugged out of the harbour his father came over and took Arvid's arm, spun him round, and it hurt, for his father was strong and his grip was tight. Arvid slipped on the deck and fell to his knees.

'Why is there always trouble with you? Why can't you be like other people just for once? Why can't you behave normally? Christ, it's as if you came from a different planet! Answer me, boy!'

Arvid stared at the planks of the deck, the yellow paint was peeling off and underneath he could see the blue coming through. There was no answer to give and his father shook Arvid's shoulder and shouted: 'Have you gone deaf? Answer me, goddamn it!' Arvid looked up. His father's face was white. He felt a knot in his stomach, like a stone and the stone grew and made everything hard and still inside him. No one could hurt him, no one could reach him, he could go wherever he wanted. He stood up, words formed in his mouth, clear as fragments of glass, but suddenly his mother was between them and the words crunched between his teeth and turned to powder.

'What are you doing? Keep away from Arvid. Have you got that? You keep well away from him!' She pushed his father in the chest and he stepped back and his mother pushed him again until he was standing with his back to the wall of the wheelhouse and he couldn't retreat any further.

The skipper stuck his head out and said: 'What's going on?' Gry took Mogens' hand and held it so hard her knuckles went white, the skipper cut the engines and came out, everyone looked at his father and there was a silence, except for the water lapping against the side of the boat. The wind was gentle and full of sea, the sun lit up the yellow boat and his father's white face. Suddenly his father was standing on the railing, holding the rigging with one hand, and he laughed.

'I'm not needed here, am I? I might just as well jump into the sea, isn't that right?'

'Don't be childish, Frank. Come back down,' his mother said. 'We can talk about this later. Don't ruin everything.'

But his father laughed. 'I might just as well jump,' he said again.

Arvid screwed up his eyes and could feel how the stone had filled him completely. 'Go on, jump then,' he said in a low voice, but everyone heard him and turned. 'Just jump. I'll help you out. I can swim like a fish. Just jump!'

His father looked down into the water and back at Arvid, he bit his lip and his face slowly turned red.

'So jump then!' Arvid shouted. 'It's not dangerous. Just jump! Don't you see you have to? You can't just *say* it and do nothing!'

His father held one hand to his face, he seemed unsteady now and scared and when he climbed down it was as if from a great height. He walked across the deck like a drunk. The skipper started the engine, the boat was shaking and his father's whole body was shaking too and

131

then his mother put her arms around him and held him tight. Gry burst into tears and Mogens stroked her hair, leaned over and whispered into her ear.

When they docked at the jetty Arvid jumped ashore at once. He was about to run, but his father came after him and grabbed him by the shoulder.

'Hang on, Arvid.'

Hands off!' he shouted, tore himself free and quickly walked along the footpath. He could hear them behind him, but he didn't listen to what they were saying any more, it was just noise and he took his bike from the stand by the beach hut, got on it and pedalled on to the road. When he had enough speed up he let go of the handlebars. When that went well he closed his eyes. At first there was a nasty bang against the wheel and he realised he was too close to the kerb, so he leaned over to the right and then the bike was in the middle of the road. Now he just listened. He heard the wind and the gulls screaming and the distant putter of a tractor in a field far off and small birds in the poplars, there had to be hundreds of them, and then he heard a car. Not very loud at first, but it was coming closer and closer behind him, and it gave him a shock when it hooted. The bike lurched, he grabbed the handlebars, still with his eyes closed, there was the scream of brakes and he felt a startling blow to the body and he thought, if I hold the handlebars tight and I don't open my eyes, I can cycle all the way to Italy.